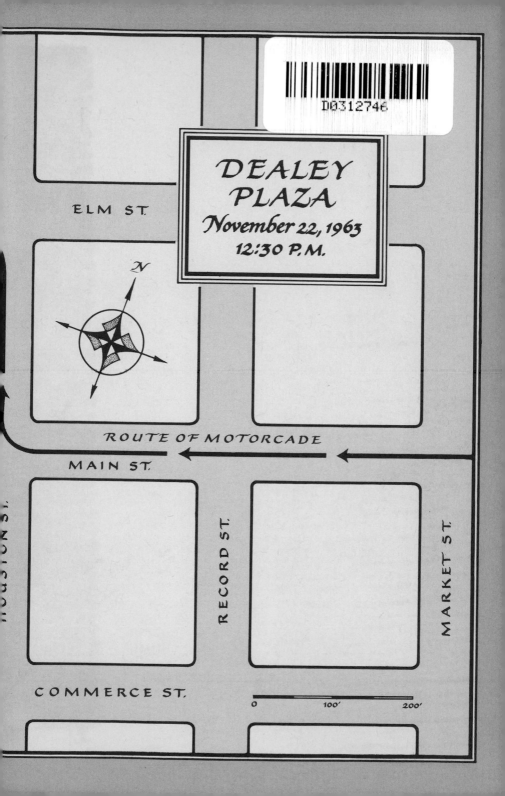

Sherlock Holmes in Dallas

EDMUND AUBREY

DODD, MEAD & COMPANY
NEW YORK

1 2 3 4 5 6 7 8 9 10

Library of Congress Cataloging in Publication Data

Ions, Edmund S
  Sherlock Holmes in Dallas.

  I. Title.
PZ4.I62Sh 1980 [PR6059.05] 823'.914 80–15980
ISBN 0–396–07904–0

Author's Note

The main sources for the author, as for Sherlock Holmes, were the 26 Volumes of Evidence and Exhibits, together with the Report of the Warren Commission investigating the assassination of President John F. Kennedy in 1963. I extend my thanks to the British Library for extended loan of the volumes in 1978, and for other research materials. Further sources included Hearings from Senate and House Committees into the activities of the CIA before and after the death of President Kennedy, and the 12 Kennedy volumes of Hearings and Appendices of the House Select Committee on Assassinations (1979). I also record my thanks to the National Archives in Washington, D.C., for assistance in viewing other materials, including the Zapruder film of the assassination, and a number of photographic slides.

Every deduction by Sherlock Holmes in this account of his last case can be documented from the above sources, but the reader will see that the renowned sleuth gives an extra dimension to the reasoning processes he brings to the case.

I had not seen my friend Holmes for some little time, and began to wonder about his health. I did not wish to impose my presence by calling at Baker Street, in case he was in one of his dark moods. These sometimes lasted for weeks at a time, and he would not be available to visitors, however eminent the client or whatever the urgency of the case. At these times, I knew well, he would lock his door and divide his day between poring over his microscope, playing the violin he kept in a corner of his sitting room, or sitting in his old armchair, puffing at his meerschaum and gazing into the embers of the fire. Only Mrs. Hudson, his devoted housekeeper, was allowed to enter, with his meals.

I was surprised, therefore, to encounter my friend suddenly, and quite unexpectedly, at a Turkish bath in Jermyn Street. Perhaps, like myself, he had noticed in *The Times* that the old building, in all its Egyptian revival splendor, was shortly to be demolished in favor of a new hotel, or some other more lucrative excrescence. The familiar voice greeted me through the steam, and I observed my old friend seated on the marble slab, swathed in a towel that clung to his lean frame. Age was beginning to tell. The hair was thinning markedly above the tall brow, and the aquiline nose looked almost beaklike, the cheeks a shade cadaverous. Even so, the eyes gleamed through the murk, and I could tell at once that Holmes had something on his mind as I settled next to him. We spent some minutes on pleasantries, during which I learned that Holmes was still taking an occasional case. Suddenly he asked,

"What would you say to a trip to America, Watson? Would you be free?"

I was quite startled by the suggestion, and could not think what he intended.

"Another encounter with the Mafiosi, Holmes?" I asked. I had in mind the Long Island case of some years ago, which Holmes had docketed as "The Case of the Naples Syndicate." Memories of its more gruesome details brought an involuntary shudder. I also recalled that Holmes had been assured, in sundry communications by telegram, and on one occasion by transatlantic telephone, that he was a marked man if ever he set foot in America again. In the strange argot employed by the villains, some of whom he helped to put in jail for life, it was conveyed that a "contract" had been served on my companion. I feared for his safety if he should be taking up another similar case.

"If the case is in New York City . . ." I began, but Holmes interrupted me.

"Not New York, my dear Watson. I share your distaste for the less salubrious sections of Manhattan and Long Island. Our journey would involve a visit to Washington, D.C., and to the city of Dallas, in Texas. It involves opening an old case."

At the mention of that city, a number of presentiments

—2

stirred in my mind. Holmes guessed at the source of my reverie. Once more he knew my thoughts even before I could compose a reply. He did not need to refer to that infamous deed which struck down a President in his prime.

"I should stress, Watson, that I have not accepted the case. Indeed, I am very much in two minds. I should like to discuss it with you before accepting, since it is an impossible commission, without a shadow of doubt."

I could see that Holmes meant what he said. Why, then, was he giving it any further consideration? I put the question to him.

"It has never been my habit to accept a case for the sole reason that I had every confidence in my ability to solve it, Watson. You will recall the case of the Hampshire Militiaman, and the Dover Castle case?"

Certainly I recalled that in both cases the culprit had escaped the clutches of the law, but I reminded my companion that his deductions had been correct in explaining the nature of the crime, besides indicating the true culprit. Only the tardiness of the law had allowed the miscreants to go scot-free.

"But I confess," Holmes continued, "that I am genuinely of two minds. I would like your advice, Watson. As you know, the crime occurred a good many years ago. Much, indeed most, of the evidence is simply no longer obtainable. Many of the key witnesses are dead. The person accused was himself shot dead within two days of the crime. And, as you know, regicide traditionally begets rumors, tales of conspiracies. But let us talk. Can you come to my rooms tomorrow in the forenoon?"

I readily assented. Despite his many caveats, I had

observed the familiar gleam in my companion's eye. I felt sure the old hunting instinct had been aroused and that he would accept the commission.

When I called next morning, Holmes was sunk in his chair. He roused himself as I entered, emptied the ash from his pipe into the coal scuttle, and motioned me to a seat. Then he handed me a letter from a sidetable. The letterhead bore a Washington address. A glance at the several signatories to the letter gave a momentary thrill. The names were among the most eminent in the United States. Some of the persons subscribed were familiar from the front pages of national newspapers on both sides of the Atlantic. I read the proposal slowly, and prepared to speak. Holmes anticipated my remark with his usual percipience.

"I know what you are about to say, my dear Watson. That I cannot refuse this commission."

I confessed that he had taken the words out of my mouth.

"But I *can* refuse if it seems to me, beyond a peradventure, that I am bound to let these people down; that there is no possibility of meeting their request."

I remonstrated. "My dear Holmes, they are not asking you to solve the case or to offer a complete explanation of what occurred, nor even to fix the blame. They merely ask your assistance in throwing any light you can on a baffling problem that has occupied able minds in two continents for many years now—some of them in public life and of the utmost eminence and perspicacity." I gestured with the letter in my hand. Holmes motioned with his long, lean hand.

"I must repeat, Watson. There is little, if anything, I

can do at this remove. Too many avenues are closed. They are choked with the weeds of time. Moreover, there is a more fundamental difficulty. You recall what I have said to you about my methods. They principally involve deduction, so as to narrow down the number of possible suspects. But in this case—who knows? It may be two, five—it may be fifty or more."

"They do not say so, Holmes. They merely wish to inquire if you are disposed to accept the official verdict, or whether, on investigation, you might possibly conclude that other persons were directly involved in the killing."

Holmes sprang from his chair. I knew that I had scored a point. He thrust his hands into the pockets of the houndstooth trousers he wore when *en pantoufles* in his rooms, and strode to the window. The gravity of the case had borne itself in upon me during the hours of the preceding night, and I now pressed home my entreaties. A clear memory of something Holmes said in the Case of the Reigate Squires came to my mind. I had carefully recorded the words in my notebook at the time. I repeated them now to my companion.

"You will recall, Holmes, that you once observed to me: It is of the highest importance in the art of detection to be able to recognize, out of a number of facts, those which are incidental and those which are vital. Surely that applies here with particular force, given the mass of testimony?"

"I recall it," Holmes said swiftly. "The Reigate Squires." I marveled again at his prodigious memory and inclined my head in acknowledgment.

Holmes had seized a pipe from the windowsill and was

stuffing an aromatic Grosvenor shag into the briar. He clutched the amber between his teeth as he came back to the hearth.

"Your view, Watson, is that I should accept the commission and put my thoughts to the matter?"

"I feel you have a duty, Holmes," I replied.

"You will accompany me?"

"I would be honored."

"Excellent." Holmes clapped his hands together, and I realized now that he had been engaging in one of his little exercises. The purpose of his reservations was not so much to assuage his doubts as to confirm a decision he had already made in his own mind. He had merely pressed me to the limits, and perhaps he wanted a companion. His next words confirmed my suppositions.

"The case is extremely complex. I have spent the last few days in the British Museum. As you may know, Watson, there is an official Report on the assassination. The Warren Report. I suggest you read it. You may borrow my copy."

He handed me a weighty tome. It bore a gold seal on the dark blue covers, and a momentary glance revealed that the Report extended to some 888 pages. Holmes's next words were more reassuring.

"You can make do with the Report. There are twenty-six volumes of testimony and exhibits to accompany it. I have studied them, but I will spare you that chore. There is no time. And many books besides, some of them serious, detailed investigations, with scholarly apparatus and a scrupulous regard for the rules of evidence. Others meretricious, mere potboilers. I have read the former and glanced more swiftly at the latter in the British Museum this last week."

"When do you wish to leave, Holmes?" I asked.

"Next Monday. The clients insist that we travel first class. They ask us to pay a call in Washington to discuss the matter, and then fly on to Texas. That will be convenient, as I wish to peruse some materials in the National Archives at Washington."

I assured Holmes that I could put my affairs in order for an absence of some days. My physician's practice could be looked after by my partner. I was keen to go. As I took my leave, Holmes held up a cautionary hand.

"I need hardly add, Watson, that the case must be treated with the utmost confidentiality."

I was reminded suddenly of the Case of the Illustrious Client.

"My lips are sealed, Holmes," I replied.

"Excellent, Watson. You are a tower of strength. Some special arrangements have been made for our transportation in the United States. A section of the Foreign Office will be assisting at certain points, but discreetly. There may be moments when I cannot divulge all the details of what I am about, or the nature of some visits, or visitants. I trust it will not try your patience if I am not at liberty to make you entirely *au courant.*"

"Not at all, my dear Holmes. We both appreciate that there are times when it is better, and safer, that vital information should be lodged with one person only."

"Capital, Watson. I am most obliged. We will meet at Heathrow Airport. All travel arrangements will be completed for us. Bring light luggage only. Our stay will last for not more than a week. I trust less. This is my last case. I plan to retire very soon to a house I have bought in a quiet corner of Sussex. Let us hope the gentlemen in New York do not learn of our visit. I would not wish to be balked of my retirement." Holmes smiled grimly.

I tucked the bulky volume under my arm and made for the door. The next few evenings were spent principally in studying the contents and other materials Holmes passed to me. The events of that tragic weekend in a Texas city came vividly to mind as I gazed at the many photographs and plans, tracing the events from the moment the young President and his wife alighted from the President's plane, through the horror of the assassin's bullets, and so to the grubby finale when Lee Oswald was himself shot by a Dallas night club owner shortly before noon, only forty-eight hours after a foul deed had taken the President's life.

2

We met at mid-morning in the main lounge at Heathrow. Holmes was ensconced in his cape, the flaps of his deer- stalker tied up over the crown. The first hint of October chill was in the air outside. He was puffing his pipe, and, as I approached him from the flanks, he greeted me without turning. I was still intrigued by this old trick of Holmes.

"How did you guess it was me, Holmes?" I asked.

"By listening, my dear Watson. Every footfall is infi- nitely different. In weight, tempo, length, each footstep has a unique profile. Two footsteps confirm a familiar presence beyond doubt. I would hardly be a professional investigator if I was not intimately familiar with your footsteps at this stage in our association. Do sit down. Our plane will be called on the board yonder. I trust the gentleman from the American Secret Service is not to be our constant companion. I prefer to work alone, as you know."

"Which gentleman, Holmes?"

"The person in the beguiling tweeds, reading *The Times* so intently."

I followed Holmes's momentary nod. I saw a middle- aged man nearby, sitting apart, hatless, dressed in an

English tweed suit complete with waistcoat and a watch chain. His trim moustache, even his complexion, and certainly his hairstyle, perfectly conveyed an Englishman in relaxed traveling clothes.

"Did you say American, Holmes? English, surely."

"Observe his shoes, Watson. Even secret agents insist on comfortable shoes, of native origin. If the gentleman were English, he would be in brogues, with that suit and tie."

I looked. His shoes were shiny, almost lacquerlike, with thick rubber soles, and with large eyelets for the laces.

"Note the sheen, the color," Holmes added. "No British shoemaker manufactures that precise shade—a dull chocolate, nor that degree of luster, and the stitching of the welt is peculiar to America."

"Are those the only clues, Holmes?" I asked, keeping my voice low to prevent it carrying.

"Not quite. Some minutes ago he pretended to attempt *The Times* crossword—an excellent disguise, save for his manner with a ballpoint pen."

"How so, Holmes?"

"Americans handle those instruments in a manner entirely different from a middle-aged Englishman in tweeds. The Englishman would hold the pen with one hand and press the button on top of the pen with the tip of his index finger, or, equally likely, with a finger from the other hand. An American clutches the pen in one fist, thrusts his arm out to the side, and presses the button with the thumb of the same hand—all in one swift, time-saving movement. That is what our secret observer did some minutes ago."

"An observer? He appears to be deep in his newspaper."

—10

"Not quite. He has been perusing the top left corner of the same page of *The Times* for the past ten minutes. Note that the top of the page is at eye level. A slight tilt, and he can hide his face completely, or survey us as he pleases."

"Why should you think he is trailing us?"

"I did not say so. I expressed the hope that he is not. On balance, I think that it is not we who engage his attention. His gaze is fixed elsewhere—at Passport clearance through that door to his front. Ah, as I thought. . . ."

The man stood up suddenly, folded his *Times*, took up the briefcase by his side, and strode off.

"Did he detect our conversation, Holmes?" I asked.

"He did indeed. You may have noticed the receiver disguised as a hearing aid behind his left ear. An excellent instrument, manufactured in Dusseldorf: the best there is. Multidirectional and it can tune in to a conversation twenty yards away."

"He heard us, then?"

"I should say so. But I was also fairly certain that we are not his game. He would have stationed himself well behind us, against the wall probably, fifteen paces away. Of course he was irritated by my piercing his disguise. Eventually his quarry will come through that door, among the arrivals. We can forget him, Watson. Ah, I see we are called to Gate Fourteen, to embark." Holmes stood up.

Some two hours later we were flying over the Atlantic. After lunch, with a light Burgundy to assist the palate, Holmes sank down into the generous cushions of the first class cabin of the plane. I envied him his old ability to sink instantly into a slumber, though I knew that he would be aroused in an instant, every nerve on the alert, at any sudden disturbance about him. It was as if the slightest change in the atmosphere affected his nostrils in some uncanny way. Thus, despite his rhythmical breathing, I knew that Holmes was only half asleep. I called for a brandy, and after another hour fell into a light doze myself.

When I awoke, Holmes was sitting up straight, looking refreshed. I surmised that he might be at his old game, deducing an astonishing range of facts about his fellow passengers across the aisle, but, as I roused myself, he taxed me with a number of questions. This was an old routine, though on this occasion I felt decidedly out of practice.

"Watson, give me your opinion on the Report of the Warren Commission."

I moved cautiously, aware that nothing was better calculated to bring Holmes to impatience than a superficial opinion, showing limited perception or second-rate judgment. I proceeded with due reserve.

"The Commission was clearly convinced that the President was killed by a lone assassin, Lee Harvey Oswald."

"Do you share that conviction?"

I drew in my breath slightly. I could have wished that Holmes had not put the question so briskly, but he could be remorseless in pursuing his inquiries, even with an old friend.

"They make a very powerful case, Holmes. I am ready to believe that Oswald killed the President. There is an overwhelming mass of evidence, some direct, some circumstantial, all in a pattern of corroboration."

I could already detect, alas, some slight signs of impatience in my companion.

"I take it, Watson, that what you conclude is that Os-

—12

wald fired a gun from the sixth floor window of the Texas School Book Depository in Dallas at the time the President was assassinated?"

"That is so, Holmes."

"Forgive me, but that is not what you said, my dear Watson."

"What is the difference?"

"You remarked that Oswald shot and killed the President. Oswald may well have fired shots from the School Depository. But not necessarily at the President."

"My dear Holmes," I expostulated, "are you really suggesting that Oswald was merely firing random shots, with a telescopic sight, at pigeons, perhaps, at the moment the President and his entourage passed beneath the building? You surely do not suggest that?"

"I suggest nothing, my dear fellow. I am merely testing the extent of your own deductions after reading the Report. Were we to agree that Oswald did indeed fire shots from a rifle at the moment the President died, a number of explanations are possible. That he was firing at someone else. Possibly someone else in the same car. He may have been hired to do so. Or Oswald could have fired decoy shots, perhaps for a price, and without asking too many questions, on the guarantee that he would not be arrested for discharging a firearm."

"You are suggesting accomplices, Holmes?"

"Watson, I am suggesting nothing at this stage. I merely offer one or two hypotheses. I could add a dozen more—but we are concerned here with getting at the facts, not simply erecting one plausible hypothesis on the basis of some selected facts."

"Is that your view of the Warren Commission Report, Holmes?"

—13

"I think that they erred very much in that direction. In matters of regicide, the populace requires an answer, which must be clear and unambiguous. If it is not supplied, the fabric of society is imperiled. The myth breaks. The chain of authority collapses. The people cannot bear that. They demand an answer. Our brief is different. No hypothesis can be ruled out. We are only at the beginning of our inquiries, Watson. Our first prescription must be to keep our minds open: the *tabula rasa.* We must have no preconceptions. If we do, we will be drawn to certain strands of evidence, and we will neglect others. The effect will be cumulative, given the vast weight of testimony supporting the officially approved hypothesis. Recall the weighty claims of the official Report: the 552 witnesses, 3,000 reports from the law enforcement agencies, 26,000 interviews—most, it was urged, sustaining the single hypothesis."

Holmes was interrupted by an announcement over the loudspeaker system. We were approaching Dulles Airport at Washington, and were advised to fasten our seatbelts for the descent. Our flight had been smooth, but I experienced a slight thrill. A good many years had elapsed since I had sailed aboard the *Queen Mary* with Holmes to New York for the Mafia case. I hoped that the ugly tentacles of that organization had long since relinquished their threat to dispatch my companion if ever he set foot in the United States again.

We landed on time, and taxied to the airport buildings. Some curious, elephantine construction on wheels approached the vast aircraft to allow us to disgorge. As we waited near the forward exit for the mobile lounge to fasten itself to the body of the plane like a limpet,

Holmes exchanged a brief word with the pretty hostess who had attended us on our flight.

"How is the fishing in Minnesota?" he asked.

The young lady looked startled. Her bright red mouth was agape.

"Have we met before, sir?" she began.

"I have not had that pleasure," said Holmes. "But I presume your grandparents came from Norway?"

The young lady looked even more startled.

"Sir, you must be a mind reader. How could you possibly know that?"

"Alas, I have no powers of clairvoyance,' Holmes replied. "Mere surmise, I do assure you."

"But you're absolutely right. How did you know?"

"When you kindly served us lunch, I observed the many hairline scratches on your thumb and first finger. Ladies who sew garments by hand sometimes gain these, but they tend to be a great deal older than you, their eyesight impaired by age. Those who fish a great deal get similar marks from inserting fish hooks into live bait, and even more from taking the hook out of the fish's mouth or gills. As for your Norwegian ancestry, I must point out that only the Norwegians have that particular translucent blue I see in your eyes. And if you will forgive my impertinence, I see that your dark hair would be very fair but for the ministrations of modern pharmacology."

The young lady laughed.

"I guess I didn't get to the roots of the matter last time I had a rinse. A bottle brunette, yes sir. You certainly amaze me. You ought to be in the FBI, if you don't mind my saying so, sir. They could use you."

I refrained from remarking that the FBI had often called on the services of Sherlock Holmes, but further conversation was interrupted as we stepped into the capacious mobile lounge on gargantuan wheels. The young lady offered her hand to Holmes and he doffed his deerstalker.

"It's been a pleasure," she remarked, then added the word "Wow!" which I took to be an observation in the American vernacular.

As we moved silently to the airport lounge, I followed up the lady's curiosity.

"How did you light upon Minnesota, Holmes?" I asked.

"Something of a long shot, Watson. A high proportion of the Norwegian immigrants in the last century went to that State, the 'Land of a Thousand Lakes,' as it boasts itself. It reminds them of their homeland. The climate is quite severe in winter, there are pine forests, but good land between, and above all, an abundance of fish. A young lady who spends most of her time confined in the unnatural surroundings of a large tube hurtling through the sky eventually finds her greatest pleasure in getting back to peaceful, deserted lakes as far as possible removed from the noisome proximities of the world's airports. Almost elementary, my dear Watson."

As we came through the Customs Hall, a liveried chauffeur approached us. He introduced himself and handed Holmes a white envelope. Holmes read the message within, inscribed in a flowing hand on stiff, deckled paper. I observed the address as O Street, Georgetown, on the copperplate letterhead. The chauffeur took our luggage and led us to a long black motor car immediately outside the airport lounge. He held the door open, and we disposed ourselves inside the ample limousine. The windows of the car were of dark blue tinted glass, and the interior was delightfully cool after the warmth that had greeted us on the concrete apron of the airport entrance. Our journey into Washington took some thirty minutes, and we motored through attractive countryside, a trifle scorched here and there by the summer's heat. Holmes expatiated on our mission.

"I remind you again, Watson, that we cannot undertake to solve the mystery. Our clients—and they are several—accept this without question. But undoubtedly there are lingering hopes in their hearts that we may resolve their fears, or, at the very least, some of the persistent rumors. We must be careful not to give any promises. I cannot stress strongly enough that the more I studied the twenty-six volumes of testimony and exhibits of evidence in the British Museum, the more the possible leads multiplied. Never in my experience have I encountered such a profusion of clues to contradictory hypotheses. I ceased to count them when they numbered some two score or more. I must convey this as strongly as I can to our clients, or we are certain to disappoint them. The very most we can hope to do is to shed a little light, perhaps close off certain thoughts or conjectures, or indicate others. Or perhaps, if I feel unduly emboldened at the end of my career, I may indicate the direction of my thoughts."

Holmes sank back into the deep leather of the limousine, and I recognized a familiar signal. No further questions. I grasped the braided strap above my shoulder and concentrated on the scenes flitting past the tinted windows. The browns and russets of the countryside were giving way to white fences and white-frame houses behind well-trimmed lawns.

3

_____

The chauffeur brought the motor car to a halt in a quiet, tree-lined street. The houses were in a variety of styles, some white frame, of clapboard, without gardens and abutting the cobbles, others almost hidden behind trees. The house we now entered lay beyond a wrought iron gate, above two levels of terraced gardens, the domicile in warm brown brick, weathered by time. The house was Georgian in style, with a classical portico of columns in white stucco. As we ascended the short flight of brick steps to the *piano nobile* of the residence, the heavy door swung open and a dusky footman took our coats. He preceded us up a curving flight of stairs with glistening mahogany balustrade. We entered a long salon where we met a group of persons, among whom I recognized several from the frequency with which their respective likenesses had appeared in photographs in the world's press. At the center of the group was a lady of uncertain age, whose identity Holmes disclosed to me only after we left England's shores. She had eminent connections. She extended her hand and motioned us to a silk-covered couch in Regency style. About her, in easy chairs, I observed some distinguished members of the Congress of the United States of America.

Our hostess trusted that we were not fatigued by our journey. Tea was served to us from a silver salver. Holmes was not one to waste time on nonessentials and came quickly to the purpose of his mission. He set out, clearly and succinctly, the limitations imposed on his brief by the passage of time and the dispersal of evidence. Our hostess graciously conceded all of his points. Some of the eminent gentlemen present attempted to inject a greater degree of optimism into the proceedings, paying tribute to the other cases Holmes had helped to solve on this same continent, but Holmes firmly demurred. He repeated to the gathering the substance of his remarks to me as we motored through the countryside from the airport. At the end of the disquisition, the gentlemen appeared satisfied. A silver-headed Senator, who had nodded thoughtfully as Holmes outlined the difficulties of a trail long since cold, rose and offered his hand to my companion.

"If you'll excuse me, Mr. Holmes, I have to get back to the Hill to sign some correspondence due out today. It's been a pleasure, sir, and you have our complete confidence. We'll be interested in whatever you come up with."

The rest of the group rose, and took their leave. Then our hostess spoke in a quiet voice, almost sepulchral in the elegant salon.

"My good wishes are with you too, Mr. Holmes. We are asking much, much more of you than any of your former clients, and I have been reminded by friends in London that you very rarely take on a case these days."

"That is so, ma'am," Holmes replied. "I will declare frankly that your first letter came as I was putting my papers in order in preparation for my retirement. You see before you a retiring, aging sleuth whose faculties are not what they were."

The lady held up a hand in remonstrance.

"Not so, Mr. Holmes. We heard, through good friends, family friends, of your work on the Vinogradoff treasures. It was they who sang your praises when a cousin called here last year."

The lady extended her hand and we took our leave. The chauffeur drove us to a private residence placed at our disposal. It was a small, handsome house in a leafy cul-de-sac, the house in colonial brick. We were assured that the butler and cook attending to our needs could be trusted absolutely. We dined quietly, in a mood of reminiscence, then took coffee and cognac in the elegant sitting room at the rear of the house, overlooking a garden surrounded by an impenetrable hedge of beech. Holmes drummed his fingers on the leather armchair in which he reclined. Suddenly he returned to what had become a familiar theme.

"Watson," he declared, "there is no solution to this case. I have already concluded this. However lucky the dice, some residue of doubts will remain. The doubts will relate to persons, but more especially to motives. As you know, the question of motive is the prime one, and an investigation ought to start with this. But here, with this murder, the question is obscure."

"You will do no more and no less than the best you can, Holmes, as with any other case."

"Correct, my dear Watson. But you will find that I will test my hypotheses on you, and at times I will stretch your patience. You must bear with me. This is a case the likes of which I have never encountered in my entire career, which, as you know, has met with not a few conundrums."

"And not a few illustrious clients," I averred.

Holmes made a dismissive gesture.

"It is not the client, but the search for truth that impels my curiosity, Watson. Many of my clients have been of humble station, not born to the purple."

I nodded my assent. Nevertheless, I wished to put a question to Holmes that had dogged me on several occasions in the past few days. I put it now.

"Holmes," I commenced, "I have been with you on a great many cases, but I confess that I have never observed such a note of pessimism in your capacity to discover a solution. Is it that you have a presentiment of failure, or that you do not feel sufficiently engaged in a case where the scent is so cold, the clues so dispersed?"

Holmes puffed at his pipe for a moment or two, exhaling the fragrant mixture through pursed lips.

"You perceive correctly, my dear Watson, that I have a presentiment of failure. Not of complete failure, but certainly of an inability to supply final proof to our clients. Of that I have no doubt. I have reconnoitered the dimensions of the problem through my reading and reflection these past few weeks. The only question in my mind is whether or not my mission will be a complete failure. I have observed in my reading that among the legacies of the tragedy are a number of post-mortem commentaries from men of the first calibre, in which it is clear that their critical faculties have been severely impaired. Whether by the enormity of the crime or the mass of testimony to hand, I cannot judge. Perhaps both. If these learned men have faltered in their reasoning, why should I expect to do better?"

"Come come, Holmes," I remonstrated. "I recall the case of the murdered college Provost in which your deductions were pitted against the finest minds at Oxford. If I may say so, you left the Professors and Fellows somewhat breathless. I recall that a posse of eminent scholars came to bid you farewell and to offer you their thanks."

Holmes raised his hand. "An altogether different case, Watson. It simply did not occur to the members of an Oxford college that their revered head of house could be blackmailed by the manciple; that the Provost was thus compelled to lay a trap, without reckoning the low cunning of a man who had embezzled college supplies for two decades. As an outsider, I was simply not a prisoner to such local sentiments as loyalty to a head of house and complete trust in college servants. The elements were plain to an outside visitor. No, my dear Watson, this case is of a quite different dimension. First class minds have stumbled in their attempts to grapple with the available evidence."

"Could you give me examples, Holmes?"

"I will give you two examples, Watson. The commentaries are utterly clear in my mind, and can be checked, if you should have occasion to do so, to the letter."

I knew that I was about to be treated to Holmes's extraordinary powers of recall. I also surmised that he wished to go over the examples of faulty reasoning for his own purposes, perhaps to repeat some private warning to himself. I therefore prepared myself to sit silently through the soliloquy which I sensed was about to begin.

"I choose two examples of first class legal minds addressing themselves to the problem, Watson. Other commentators abound, but many are specious, some of them scandalously so, and quite irresponsible in their fanciful conjectures. I dismiss these commentaries as part of the detritus of our popular culture today. But the ones of which I speak deserve notice, since they proceed from the very best intellects for such problems—that is, the mind trained to sift and, more vitally, to weigh evidence, to distinguish between proven fact and seductive inference."

"Give me your examples, Holmes," I interjected, unable to contain my impatience.

"Let us take first of all Lord Devlin, one of the most eminent high court judges in the United Kingdom, who presided over many of the most famous cases at the Old Bailey in our era. His legal opinions have earned the highest commendation at the Bar and in the high courts. His summing up at the end of many a long-running trial, with a mass of testimony, has often been applauded by the Law Lords. But as to the case in hand, he faltered in his handling of the Report of the Warren Commission. Lord Devlin supplied a detailed commentary in an American monthly, *The Atlantic,* early in 1965, soon after the publication of the Warren Report in 1964. The same commentary was also published by the London weekly the *New Statesman* in March of 1965. Lord Devlin began by opining that since the object of the Commission was to uncover the actions of the man or men who were privy to the murder, the enquiry necessarily began with Lee Harvey Oswald as the chief suspect, and that its scope depended on whether the suspicion could be proved. Those were his Lordship's exact words. From this tendentious appraisal, Lord Devlin deduced that the first question was, inevitably—this was the word used, whether Oswald was guilty."

"Was that not so, Holmes?" I queried.

"No, my dear Watson. It was not. In a complicated case, especially a case where political, even international dimensions *could* be present, including the murky depths of espionage and counterespionage, it may well be crucial that the most obvious suspect should *not* be the first object of attention, since it could be the planned intention of the murderers that this same suspect should be subject to intensive investigation in order to provide a false trail, to lead the investigators up a blind alley so that they might exhaust themselves and feel reluctant to start on a fresh trail. Lord Devlin failed to observe that Oswald was the chief suspect because the Dallas police asserted that he was the chief suspect from the moment of the assassination—which is why they set out to arrest him, with startling alacrity, it would seem. Yet they had entirely failed to check the movements of this 'chief suspect' in the hours before the killing."

"But if my memory serves me, Holmes, Oswald killed a Dallas policeman, Police Officer Tippit, within forty-five minutes of the assassination of the President. Did that not point to his guilt?"

"That is the conclusion of Lord Devlin. He asserts that the two things hang together. But they do not; they point to a number of hypotheses, one of which may be that Oswald believed, on the spot, that he had been 'framed,' as I believe the American vernacular puts it. And that could mean that he committed the assassination, or that he did not. His reaction would be the same, in either case. We begin to enter the complexities of the case, Watson. But I continue with Lord Devlin's reasoning. He asserts in his article that there was one eyewitness who claimed to identify Oswald as the President's assassin. This was one Howard L. Brennan, and Lord Devlin opines that this witness's claim made 'a natural foundation for the case against Oswald.' But since Brennan was 120 feet from the window, and since Brennan had by that time seen Oswald's picture on television, and since, indeed, the Commission itself goes no further than to say that the man in the window closely resembled Oswald, it is not reasonable to say that Brennan's claim produced a natural foundation for the case against Oswald.

"Moreover—but this we must test at the scene of the crime, Watson—an assassin at the corner window of the Texas School Depository shortly after noon on a day of sunshine would require to aim his rifle in the glare of the sun, in a southwesterly direction. To see his target he would undoubtedly have shielded himself from the glare by standing back from the window—a very dusty window in its upper portions—even were he so foolish as to have no wish to conceal himself from the crowds below, which we might think would be an instinctive reaction in any case. You will have noted a photograph in the Commission's Report that the police reenactment of the shooting position shows the assassin to be out of direct view from the Plaza below. The weight placed on the supposed identification of Oswald at a sixth-story window becomes all the more extraordinary. Lord Devlin goes on to observe that Brennan's description of the gunman to a police officer was most probably the basis of the description circulated to all Dallas policemen only fifteen minutes after the murder. You must try to imagine for yourself how complete a description you could make of a shadowy figure appearing—if he appeared at all—for no more than a second or two, six stories aloft behind a half-open window, the upper half covered with dust, at a moment of considerable confusion as onlookers screamed, the shots still ringing with their echoes about the Plaza.

"Lord Devlin's article is fairly long, and as you would expect, closely reasoned. Herein lies a source of error. Where other explanations are possible, these are discounted if they do not support the simple, and seductive hypothesis of a solitary assassin, Oswald, with a single gun. The kernel of Lord Devlin's support of the Commission's Report is that Oswald was in the building at the time of the assassination, and that the President was killed by a gun that belonged to Oswald. As to the first point, if an employee is in a building that is his normal daily workplace this cannot in itself be grounds for suspicion. Indeed, there might be greater grounds for suspicion if he were absent from his place of work at the vital moment."

"But it was established that Oswald left his workplace immediately the President was killed?"

"It is firmly established that he was located in a cinema more than an hour after shots were fired at the President. His movements before then, during that hour, are uncertain, and there is conflicting testimony. As to the second point, we could concede that the President was killed by a rifle owned by Oswald without conceding that Oswald fired the shots."

"But Oswald's fingerprints were on the rifle, and on cartons at several points near the window in the School Depository."

"That is unsurprising. The fingerprints merely established that Oswald quite possibly handled his rifle at or about the time of the killing. It does not establish that he fired the rifle at the time and place asserted, or that Oswald aimed at the President, still less that this was the

_26

only gun at that window, or any other location. And since Oswald was an employee checking supplies, we would expect his fingerprints on cartons of books."

"Surely there was a good deal of ballistic evidence supporting the official conclusion, Holmes?"

"We must leave that for a more detailed discussion, Watson. You recall that the evidence is confusing as to the third bullet. Or again the curious case of one bullet found intact on the bloodstained stretcher in the hospital where the President died. No satisfactory explanation of this bizarre fact has been offered. That is merely one reason why we must keep an open mind. There are other reasons, but this one suffices."

"There is no doubting, surely, that Oswald was found in a cinema and that he attempted to resist arrest—indeed, that he flourished a gun at the policeman seeking to arrest him? There were several independent witnesses."

"Correct, Watson. Oswald was seen to enter a cinema, he was in a state of considerable agitation when apprehended, and independent witnesses confirm that he flourished a pistol before he was arrested. These facts do not in themselves point to any direct connection with the murder of the President some eighty minutes earlier. They *could* point to the fact that Oswald had murdered Police Officer Tippit some thirty minutes earlier, but not necessarily beyond that event. They may point only to the fact that Oswald surmised that he was being hounded by the police for a dastardly crime he did not commit. Or they may point to the fact that Oswald was not expecting to be arrested for a crime in which he was implicated but in which, correctly or incorrectly, he felt that persons in authority had promised him protection from arrest.

—27

There are further possible explanations, but these will suffice for the moment."

"Does that complete the case against Lord Devlin, if I may so put it?"

Holmes chuckled at my jest.

"Not quite, I fear. The learned Lord accepts as corroborating evidence for Oswald as the prime suspect an earlier charge against Oswald that, in April 1963, he attempted to murder an American Major General, Edwin A. Walker. The extraordinary aspect of this charge is that the evidence for it would not stand up to detailed cross-examination in any court of law. It rests very largely on a mutilated photograph alleged to have been taken at General Walker's house at the time of the attempt on his life. But the only vital detail for dating the photograph and for verifying the ownership of a car parked outside the General's house at the time—namely the license plate of the car in question—was obliterated when presented to the Commission as evidence to condemn Oswald. An eyewitness to the shooting incident had already stated to the FBI that neither of two men— *two,* mark you—leaving the scene of the crime in separate cars resembled Oswald. Even were it proved beyond a reasonable doubt that Oswald had attempted to shoot General Walker, there would be a difficulty in linking the attempt on the life of an extreme right-wing figure, notorious for his bellicose conservative views, and the later assassination of a national figure who was denounced and excoriated by those same conservative forces for his extreme liberal views, especially in the days up to and including the day of the President's death. The two attempts by the same person are not beyond the bounds of possibility, but they do not in themselves make Os-

—28

wald the prime suspect, even if a mound of evidence supported the first accusation."

"But surely, Holmes," I demurred, "the psychopath—which is what portions of the evidence established in the case of Oswald—the psychopath would not make the finer distinctions you adumbrate. He need only have a fondness, or a psychopathic need, to murder figures of authority?"

"A useful point, Watson. But Oswald was not proved to be a psychopath, and certainly not up to the moment of the assassination. Were that so, he most certainly would not have been at large in Dallas—still less at his work place on the President's route, on the day of the assassination. No, Oswald was an inadequate person first, a potential killer second, at a considerable remove. All psychopaths are inadequate in one form or other, as you know with your physician's experience, Watson; but Oswald's inadequacies fell some way short of the ability to murder in cold blood. Possibly Oswald was persuaded, or bribed, or in some way induced or compelled to act, if he aimed and fired at President Kennedy on the fatal day. If so, I do not think the idea, or the proposal, originated with Oswald. Too many psychological—and political—strands conflict with such a proposition. But I stress once more that we are only at the commencement of our investigations, Watson . . ."

I reflected for some moments on these observations, then returned to the main burden of our discussion.

"I think you make your point, Holmes, on the extraordinary way the case seems to have affected Lord Devlin—a first-rate legal mind. What of your other example?"

"Another first class intellect. Professor A.L. Goodhart, an American scholar who was Master of University College at Oxford, and showered with academic honors on both sides of the Atlantic during a career of the utmost eminence. Professor Goodhart contributed a learned article to the *Law Quarterly Review* in January 1967, under the title "The Mysteries of the Kennedy Assassination." I have a copy in my luggage which I had meant to pass to you last weekend. I will let you have it for bedtime reading to sharpen your faculties, Watson. It is a sagacious piece, on the whole, although the learned scholar is perhaps too concerned—as was Lord Devlin—to conclude that the Warren Commission had arrived at the truth, the whole truth, and nothing but the truth in the matter. One is almost disposed, at times, to see the legal profession closing ranks to bring aid and comfort to colleagues who had worked on the vast and intricate task of sifting the evidence."

"And where does Professor Goodhart err, in your opinion, Holmes?"

"In reading into some of the events on that tragic day a particular interpretation that a scholar of judicious temperament ought perhaps to avoid."

"An example, please."

"The professor asserts that critics of the Dallas police fail to note how efficient the police were after the assassination. That in little more than an hour, Oswald was arrested in the cinema. But as we have noted in some of our cases in England and on the continent, Watson, extreme efficiency in the police force may sometimes point to some form of predetermination, or prior knowledge of the suspect's whereabouts in the confusion of a city where scores of thousands of people are moving about their errands in a thousand different directions."

"But it could, equally, mean that the Dallas police were

more efficient than usual because of a special state of alertness all that day, especially after the enormity of the crime was announced over police car radios?"

"Excellent, Watson!" exclaimed Holmes. "That is exactly the riposte I had hoped for. It demonstrates that you have begun to atune your mind to our special task on this occasion: the omnipresent alternative hypothesis." Holmes smote his thigh to stress the point.

"What other shortcomings did you observe in this learned article?" I continued.

"The article is, in effect, a critical review of two works on the Report of the Warren Commission. Mr. Mark Lane's book *Rush To Judgement* and Mr. Epstein's book entitled *Inquest,* both extant in 1966, and both of which found serious fault with the work of the Warren Commission. The main burden of Professor Goodhart's article is that the Commission did indeed reach the correct conclusion—that Oswald was the killer and that Oswald acted alone. He asserts that Mr. Lane indulges in dangerous and fantastic conspiracy theories to account for the President's death, whilst Mr. Epstein posits an accomplice. As to the first item, the identity of the killer, Dr. Goodhart points out that Oswald was in the Texas School Depository at the time of the killing, and that he left the building before it was sealed off. To accept this strand of evidence without further question is a principal step to accepting the main conclusions of the Warren Commission, even though it would not necessarily follow that if Oswald was indeed in the Book Depository at the time of the killing, that he was a lone assassin, or even that he acted in complicity with any other person or persons there at that time.

"As to conspiracy theories, the learned Master dismisses such possibilities. But the main thrust of his argument is that these must be dismissed for reasons of state. They can only do harm to the United States government, or to international understanding. Those who believe in conspiracy theories are eager to cast discredit on the United States, the professor averred. But no such conclusion is warranted, any more than the opposite conclusion by critics of the Commission that it was, in American parlance, a "whitewash" for the FBI, the Dallas police, or perhaps for the Intelligence community in the United States."

"Are you saying there *was* a conspiracy, Holmes?" I interjected.

"I am not, my dear Watson. Bear in mind my earlier injunction. We are to keep our minds open. I am saying that a conspiracy was not impossible, as part of the explanation for the President's death. In dismissing all conspiracy theories at the end of his article because no compelling evidence of one had been presented, our learned professor made the error of confusing what must be proved in law beyond a reasonable doubt—most often in order to establish guilt or innocence—and what we might term historical truth: an interpretation acceptable to the dispassionate, reasonable man on the balance of the available evidence after careful deductions."

Holmes yawned suddenly. He looked at his timepiece.

"It is late, and I must be about in good time tomorrow for my work at the National Archives." He rose.

"Are there some further materials bearing on the case you wish to study?" I asked.

"There are indeed," my companion replied. "Not merely the actual exhibits portrayed in the twenty-six volumes of evidence produced by the Warren Commission, but a good deal of evidence beyond these. I have been given special permission to see some of those under the legislation that allows American citizens to claim a 'right to know.' As you are aware, Watson, there's nothing like getting the feel of a case from the available clues."

I knew what Holmes meant. How often had I seen him with the magnifying glass, his meerschaum clamped between those thin, ascetic lips, sniffing the actual aroma of a piece of cloth, or wetting his thumb and placing it along the edge of a knife, or axe, or some other dastardly weapon. Holmes found these tangible experiences invaluable for scenting new leads—very often in a literal sense—as if some olfactory residue was present.

"I bid you goodnight, Watson," my friend said briskly.

"Goodnight, Holmes." Soon after, I put out the lights, and in my bedroom took a sleeping potion in order to sleep soundly for the exhausting days I expected would lie beyond the morrow.

4

Our departure for Texas was delayed by a day, as Holmes required more time at the National Archives. I occupied my time beneath the domes of the vast art gallery that the Republic had raised to house the nation's art treasures—assisted by an unusual subvention, I was told, by a Mr. Mellon. Holmes arrived back at our grace and favor residence soon after six in the evening. He was not in a communicative mood, and I knew well enough that it was better not to disturb his thoughts.

Next day, we departed for Texas and flew southwest over the Virginia countryside toward the broad plains and farmland of the American Middle West. After a while, my companion roused himself and I could detect that he was not averse to a question.

"Did your researches prove fruitful?" I ventured. It was the first time I had touched on the matter.

"Possibly, Watson. It is too early to say. There is both too much evidence and too little. I trust we will not have to continue our journey beyond Dallas, to New Orleans, or to Chicago, or perhaps to Miami. I do not relish the peculiar pleasures of that resort, as you know."

Indeed, I knew well. I recalled the time, some ten years earlier, when Holmes had made a direct flight, at very short notice, from London to Miami to assist in the grue-some Coral Gables murders investigation, in which a villainous crew named the Coconut Grove Syndicate was implicated. That visit, too, had been extended when the trails led back to an insalubrious region of New Jersey. I knew that Holmes would not wish to extend his inquiries beyond our present destination. I could see that the possible dimensions of the case continued to induce in him a mood of gloomy presentiment.

We landed near Fort Worth in Texas after an excellent luncheon fortified by a Californian wine that wrung praises from my colleague. There was a slight delay for disembarkation after the high-pitched note of the engines had stopped. As we stood with our hand luggage, the stewardess standing next to Holmes complimented him on his headgear.

"I like the hat. Would that be what they call a deer-stalker, sir?"

"It would indeed," replied Holmes, "though I confess that I have never engaged in that particular sport."

"Oh, but you're English," said the young lady. "That's cute. I'm hoping to go there next vacation. I'm looking forward to London."

"I'm sure you will enjoy it," observed Holmes. "It should be quite a change from riding in rodeos."

The young lady started.

"Have we met before, sir? I don't remember you."

"I think not."

"Well, how do you know about my craze?"

"Your left hand, madam. As you served us luncheon, I noticed that the skin on your thumb and forefinger is hard—slightly calloused in fact. I have met it before in men who spend much time in the saddle, using the reins in the familiar manner, but leaving the right hand free for the lasso, when catching young cattle on the run."

The stewardess held up her hand.

"Right!" she exclaimed, with a merry chuckle. "Just look at those callouses! But what about rodeos? How did you figure that one?"

"Your suntan omits a fine pale line on the cheeks, on either side of the chin, if you will forgive a personal observation, where the sun has not penetrated. One sees it in Spain and in South America on the gauchos who ride horses whilst ranching and secure their headgear with a leather thong around the chin. I imagine that you spend some of your time sitting beneath the glare of the Texas sunshine."

"Right on!" said the young lady, in a strange idiom I had not encountered before. "But how did you know I'm Texan? On this airline I could be from anywhere."

"I observed you getting your personal effects ready from the vestibule as we were preparing to land. Your luggage told me a great deal, especially the family presents from Europe. Then there is your name. . . ."

The young lady looked down at the inscription on her tunic. SUE GRETCHEN.

"A German name, I believe," Holmes remarked. "And Texas is very strong in German-American stock. There were other clues, but allow me to keep one or two observations to myself."

"Gee!" exclaimed the young lady. "You must be from that place—what do they call it, Scotland Yard?"

"I have been there," Holmes replied, with what I knew to be a considerable degree of understatement, "but I am glad to say that it is not my regular employ."

The door of the cabin swung open, allowing the glare

of sunlight to penetrate. We bade our young hostess farewell, and descended to the tarmac. As we came through the arrivals hall, a uniformed chauffeur touched his cap and reached for our luggage.

"You must be Mr. Sherlock Holmes, sir? I'm detailed to meet you and take you to your hotel. Is this Dr. Watson? How do you do, sir. This way, if you please." His voice was unmistakably English.

Soon after, we were finding our way around a commodious penthouse suite in a large modern hotel in the city of Dallas. We signed the hotel register under incognitos, as Holmes prescribed. Holmes strolled out to the balcony and looked down at the traffic. Our bedrooms lay on either side of a large sitting room *en suite.* Holmes came in and stretched out on a leather sofa, kneading a mixture of his favorite tobacco into the bowl of his pipe.

"Tomorrow, Watson," he said, as he puffed away, "we walk through Dealey Plaza at exactly the time the crime took place. I will be spending part of the morning at the municipal library, going through issues of the local newspapers for the days preceding the President's death."

"To get the feel of the place at that time," I observed. I recognized one of Holmes's settled techniques of investigation.

"Precisely, Watson. And for anything incidental or unexpected one might encounter in the pages. I doubt that there will be, but you will recall that the chief suspect, Oswald, was an avid newspaper reader. There is the famous photograph—a rifle in one hand, newspapers in the other. Radical journals, if the snapshot was truthful, but there is other testimony to the fact that Oswald's reactions were sometimes affected by the newspapers. A small item, but it could be important. We must discover what he was likely to be reading in the local press, especially in the two or three days before the killing. He would need at least that time to prepare any plan, but probably more than that—assuming that he was the assailant."

"You still entertain doubts on that matter, Holmes?" I queried.

"Neither doubts nor convictions, Watson. As I have observed several times now"—at which point he wagged his finger at me gently—"we keep our minds open. Not merely for the alternative hypothesis—any second-rate detective is trained to do that—but for a multiplicity of hypotheses. In that way, we minimize the possibility of excluding other leads that may guide us toward the truth, or at least to some approximation of the truth. Which is all we can hope for, let us continue to remind ourselves."

I nodded my assent.

"We will dine here tonight, Watson. We must be careful not to be seen too much. Our chauffeur was supplied by a special authority, from Washington sources, and we are assured of his absolute discreetness. But I would not wish to be recognized, least of all by the local press. Keep your new name securely in mind, together with mine, in case of sudden questions if we happen to be apart during our visit."

I nodded. I had already spent much of our flight from Washington memorizing the details. Holmes was Mr. Hammond, a British architect interested in urban renewal problems. I was his partner in a London practice, a Mr. Elliott. Holmes's contacts with the Foreign Office had obligingly furnished us with the necessary accoutrements, from headed writing paper to membership cards of Architects' Associations, in order to preserve our incognitos.

Our assumed profession would be valuable for our peregrinations, Holmes had observed wryly. He was already squinting through the small theodolite he had brought with him, measuring the vertical angles between the cornice of the sitting room and various items of furniture. He had used the instrument in another case, to measure the trajectory of a missile.

I took a leisurely bath in the windowless sepulchre attached to my bedroom, with its abundance of white, furry towels, supplied with prodigality in a manner common to American hostelries.

Holmes rang for room service as we sat on the balcony a little later, looking at the westering sun sinking beneath the harsh lines of tall buildings. A page boy appeared within the minute. Holmes ordered from the dinner menu, and I did so in turn.

"Yes, Mr. Hammond," the page said. I was briefly taken aback by the name, but my passing confusion was covered by Holmes's further instructions for evening and morning newspapers to be delivered to our suite.

We dined well, the T-bone steak all that one had expected in this homeland of American beef: gargantuan, by our more modest standards in Europe, but succulent nonetheless. After dinner Holmes stretched out on the sofa, reading the evening newspaper for a while, as I read the Tolstoy I had brought with me for the trip. For a few moments Holmes switched on the gleaming white television set that protruded from the wall on an angular metallic arm. He moved through the various stations fairly rapidly, the switch producing small plosive sounds in the suite. Garish colors exploded on the screen. Holmes emitted a low note of disgust, then switched off the machine, pushing it to the wall in evident distaste. "As one feared. A somewhat brash city given over to Mammon," he observed. At his rooms in London, Holmes had still not succumbed to this modern vice, but I recognized the familiar process of testing the local atmosphere, the prevailing spirit of place.

We retired early. Happily the double thickness of glass on the windows kept out most, though by no means all the strange whooping noises of police cars as they sped about, no doubt pursuing the criminal element in this strange, restless city whose very atmosphere seemed to breathe some menace.

5

Holmes was awake early. When I joined him for breakfast, served in our suite, I could see that he had already been at work, making notes, at the small writing table by the sliding windows giving out to the balcony. His old zest for the chase was back, the sharp eyes hawklike in their deep sockets. After a light breakfast of coffee and rolls, he flung down his napkin and strode off to his room. It was not yet 9 o'clock.

"I must be off, Watson. We will meet at noon at the north corner of Dealey Plaza, where Houston Street meets Elm Street."

We checked over a street map at the writing table, and agreed on the precise location.

"Here," said Holmes, tapping the map, "is the Texas School Book Depository. I am obtaining entry under my architect's identity. Whether I shall get to that ill-famed location on the sixth floor I can only conjecture. Now, I must consult the newspaper files." With that, Holmes was off.

I glanced at the morning newspapers, then gazed out over the city from the balcony. The early morning mist was lifting, the sun appearing fitfully through clouds. I put on a light mackintosh, placed personal documents in my suitcase, as Holmes had instructed, and revolved the three brass counters to jumble the code. I felt that I could best assist Holmes by a reconnoiter of the terrain where the assassination had occurred, and accordingly I strolled there at mid-morning. I proceeded northward along Houston Street, until the ugly building of the School Book Depository stood opposite. Here, Houston Street was bisected by the sharp left turn of Elm Street going west, past a low knoll, studded with trees, to where a triple underpass gathered Elm Street, Main Street, and Commerce Street together to sweep out to the freeway beyond. The acute angle of the bend from Houston to Elm Street struck me forcibly. Whoever planned the route of the motorcade should have recognized that the long Presidential car would be forced to slow down almost to a halt as it negotiated that acute bend. Did someone blunder? I glanced up at the Book Depository. It was clear that the killer, or killers, had an ideal eyrie, whether the intention was to shoot the President from behind or from the front. To shoot from the front as the cars approached the depository northward up Houston Street, with a bevy of Secret Service men scanning the horizons to the fore, would of course have invited instant detection. Shots from behind, once the limousine had turned down Elm Street, would be a natural choice to induce general confusion. The locale chosen, together with the selected trajectory for a car moving slowly toward an underpass, suggested a degree of shrewd planning and expert knowledge.

I found myself at this stage deliberately adopting the plural form when surmising at the agents of the assassination, and I adopted the plural form in discoursing on my thoughts from this moment on, in order to meet

Holmes's injunctions. However, I still attempted to keep Holmes's main advice constantly in mind: to assume neither one assassin, nor two, nor several implicated in the plot. In short, to presume nothing.

I walked down Elm Street and ascended the grassy knoll above the curve of the road where the President met his end. It was the ordinariness, indeed the architectural mediocrity of this place that bore most urgently on my senses. Surely, one pondered, that vigorous young tribune should not have died amidst this tasteless facade of concrete, these mundane office blocks and ugly edifices?

Soon after noon, I observed Holmes striding toward me at our rendezvous. He looked somber and, as he slackened his pace to match mine, I saw that he had been somewhat affected by his morning's work. I asked him if it had been profitable.

"I read the newspaper files for the days before the President's visit. They make ugly reading, Watson. I shall speak of them later. But I do not doubt that when the President arrived at Dallas on that fateful day, this city contained many—perhaps many thousands—who loathed him and all that he stood for. One newspaper editorial at least may have much to answer for, but that is idle speculation, needless to say."

"You imply, Holmes, that the tone of a newspaper could have contributed to the tragedy?"

"Impossible to say. But if some demented creature felt driven to murder the President, he would have done so in the knowledge that at least one important newspaper in this city—its editor and thus, perhaps, its readers—would not be averse to the deed, however accomplished."

"Does this assist the Oswald thesis?"

"It assists it if Oswald was filled with hate and also wished to make his mark in history. But if the official thesis is correct, we need to explain why he attempted so strenuously to elude capture. The official Report argues that he was ready to kill a policeman to escape recognition and retribution. This does not suggest a search for glory, though he could have panicked. In any case, Watson, as your own profession so constantly tells you, the innermost recesses of motivation—especially among those with disturbed minds—defy the reasoning processes of more orderly minds. Let us look at the terrain."

Holmes had brought some binoculars, and these he used discreetly, with short, sharp scrutinies of the Plaza, the buildings surrounding it, and the School Book Depository. This building he perused from a variety of angles and distances. Once or twice he jotted down an observation in the small notebook he was carrying in his jacket. Eventually, as we stood on the grassy knoll, looking northward to the School Depository, and across the Plaza to Houston Street, running north to south, I could contain my impatience no longer.

"Have you any new hypothesis, Holmes?"

"Not yet, Watson. Merely questions, for which I can find no satisfactory answer."

"May I know some of them?"

"The direction of the motorcade. It came down Main Street, the thoroughfare bisecting Houston Street. It then turned north, traveled no more than a few yards, then turned west on Elm Street, an exceedingly difficult turn to negotiate. The route was chosen principally to give easier access to the freeway to the west, although traffic could quite easily have been diverted for a brief period in order to give access to the freeway in a much more direct manner—thus avoiding these difficult turns. The grassy knoll where we stand would occur to any ordinary person as an unusual source of danger to a President. So is the underpass, if the motorcade has been slowed down in order to negotiate these turns. This should surely have occurred to those who spent much time planning possible routes for distinguished visitors to the city. The President was hardly the first important political figure with political enemies to visit Dallas. The short westward loop of Elm Street, passing a knoll with a scattering of trees and bushes, strikes me as a dangerous point, to say the least. However, Watson, hindsight is always easy, coming after events. We must allow that the Dallas police, the FBI agents, and the other security men planning the route did not anticipate what was to occur. This portion of the route must remain a curiosity —especially as the police cordon covering buildings on Main Street appears to have thinned out markedly just short of the Texas School Book Depository. A tragic shortcoming, in the event."

We had strolled on until we were beneath a cluster of trees some yards from the unlovely building, now of odious legend, at the corner of Houston and Elm Streets. I had expected to accompany Holmes into the Book Depository if we were allowed to enter, but he now announced a stratagem that brought me a measure of disappointment, even though I readily acquiesced with his proposal. It appeared that his hosts in Washington had arranged an assignation for Holmes not far from where we were standing. Only in this way could he hope to effect entry.

"My apologies and my regrets, Watson, but two Englishmen might strike the Superintendent as a trifle suspicious. It will be difficult enough to effect entry for one. I am sure you understand. Let us meet at the hotel later. I will acquaint you with the details."

I made my way back, and although less than an hour must have elapsed, it seemed an eternity. I drank chilled vermouth on the balcony of our suite at the top of the hotel. The scrape of the key in the lock brought me instantly to my feet. Holmes entered, and I detected that there had been some minor gain, some slender advance in the intricate mental patterns he had been weaving since our first discussions at his rooms in Baker Street.

Holmes flung himself into a deep armchair.

"My apologies to you once more, Watson," he began. "My intercessor this morning was an American, as you may have surmised."

"I am intrigued by what you hoped to accomplish, Holmes."

"I know you are, Watson. I will be brief. My contact this morning purported to be what is termed here an 'elevator inspector.' As we would put it in England, a man who inspects the lifts for safety. He had all the right papers, signed and sealed. We inspected the lifts—the elevators, as we must learn to say in this country—very thoroughly. The Superintendent was most helpful, and left us alone, so that we could test at each floor. My companion enabled me to make a quick reconnoiter of several floors."

"But surely you encountered other people at work, Holmes?"

"We chose an opportune time. By 12:30, almost all had gone off for lunch. The one or two we met were hard at work, and not surprised. My companion had other papers to establish his *bona fides,* as well as a valuable, bureaucratic aspect to his countenance."

"Did you make any startling discoveries?"

"None that impel any particular conclusions at this stage. But one gets the feel of a place, as you know, Watson. And the view from the corner of the sixth floor was useful. It is always useful to stand in the footprints, so to speak, of the murderer—or murderers."

"You speak of more than one, Holmes . . ."

"I do, but I do not state this as ascertainable fact. I merely wanted to see if there was room for more than one rifle at that window on the sixth floor."

"And was there?"

"It was just possible, but highly improbable."

"What would be the import if that occurred?"

"The problem of three, or four, or more bullets in rapid fire would be solved. As you know, there has been much debate on whether the alleged murder weapon did —even whether it was ballistically capable of murdering the President by means of three rapid shots from a bolt-operated rifle."

"Any other discoveries?"

"The lifts—the elevators—were interesting. Somewhat slow. Unlikely to be used by any assassin. The stairs at the rear of each floor would be preferred for any getaway from the sixth floor. But equally, the assassin, or the assassins, would know that a valuable amount of time would elapse before any ascent. And you recall that the police found both elevators at the fifth floor, with their doors open, immediately after the assassination."

"But surely fellow workmen were about the place on that day? Any one of them could have used the elevators."

"True, but very few, given the lunch hour break. The President's car happened to pass the Book Depository at 12:30 P.M., almost on time. Oswald could not have asked for a more propitious moment to fire his shots, and then to make a safe getaway. That is, if he hoped for, or was promised, a safe getaway."

"If, that is, he fired those shots," I put in.

"Capital, my dear Watson! You do well to check that particular conjecture. But you observe the curious bout of coincidences that came together in this crime? We are some way from our goal, Watson. After lunch, we will be taking a bus."

"A bus?" I was ready to remonstrate. My dim memories of taking a bus with Holmes for some thirty blocks of Fifth Avenue in New York in the case of the art theft at the Metropolitan Museum of Art were none too happy. Surely our clients were willing to reimburse us for a taxi cab?

"It is believed that Oswald took a bus when he left the School Book Depository. We must do the same. Then we will be going out to a place called Irving, some fifteen miles distant. I fear you are not going to enjoy the afternoon, Watson. We may even have to sit in a cinema." Holmes chuckled. He knew that I could not abide cinemas. I remembered the case of the Soho Syringe Murders—a vile series of crimes where innocent victims were despatched in complete silence, whilst others sat watching the flickering screen. That unsavory case obliged us to sit in cramped Soho cinemas on summer afternoons, witnessing insalubrious encounters on celluloid.

"Very well, Holmes," I observed gloomily. "I know that there will be a reason."

"Excellent, Watson. Now if you would kindly press the

bell for lunch, I will allow my thoughts to wander on some puzzling aspects of the case."

We settled to our meal after the waiter had returned the chafing dishes to the electric hotplate. When he had departed, Holmes ate in silence for some minutes. I surmised that he was thinking carefully and logically through some course of events, trying to fit an explanation to them. This was indeed so.

"In a complex case such as this, Watson," he began suddenly, "where there is an overwhelming mass of evidence, some of it bearing on the crime, some of it peripheral, much of it irrelevant, we must look for isolated facts, verbal incidents, remarks, observations, which may point to some pattern of events, even where that pattern is at variance with the accepted explanation of the crime."

"Do you have examples from the present case?" I queried.

"Nothing that forms a pattern. But there are some puzzling features that do not fit the received explanation that Lee Harvey Oswald acted alone, his actions sparked primarily, and at short notice, by the collapse of his marriage. His matrimonial difficulties may well have contributed to a wish to assassinate a glamorous President. The question is whether that would be a sufficient rather than a necessary explanation."

"And what are these inexplicable incidents you have in mind, Holmes?"

"They are separated in time and place, but one is forced to conjecture at their explanation. For instance, it is established that in the early March of 1963, Lee Oswald bought a high-powered rifle by mail order from a sporting goods shop in Chicago, under the assumed name of 'A. Hidell.' Why did he use a fictitious name? The obvious explanation is clearly that someone who had often expressed sympathy with a foreign Communist power, who had lived in Russia for a time, and who had brought back a Russian bride, preferred to keep such a purchase secret in case it aroused suspicions. In that case, however, Oswald must surely have recognized that he would arouse even more suspicion. He knew that he was under surveillance by the FBI, and that any attempt to practice with the gun would be noted, and questions would be asked. It was no sort of offense for Oswald to purchase such a weapon—least of all in the State of Texas, where a very high proportion of the population keep firearms—some for self-protection, many more for weekends of shooting fauna in the wild. Oswald was thus inviting police and FBI inquiries on one aspect—an assumed name—that was well designed to arouse suspicions on the other, lawful aspect, the purchase of a gun. Of course, there is that well-known facet of the criminal mentality known to you and your colleagues in the medical profession—the subconscious desire to be apprehended—and I do not discount this. Still, the incident remains puzzling. Moreover, I have not been able to trace any evidence that Oswald enjoyed shooting wild animals, or that this was one of his pastimes. The reasons for the purchase remain obscure."

"Self-protection, then?"

"One does not buy a high-powered rifle with telescopic sights for self-protection. It is cumbersome, one cannot carry it on public transport or when walking abroad, nor can it be used swiftly if one is disturbed at home by marauders. No, Watson, a pistol is the obvious choice as a weapon of self-defense—easily carried, and concealed, ready for instant use in any emergency. Moreover, Oswald later bought a .38 Smith & Wesson revolver using the same assumed name. He kept it in his furnished room in Dallas, or so the police investigations established. The rifle, however, was kept at a house in the suburb of Irving, some miles away, where his wife was living. It was stored in the garage, concealed in a blanket among seabags and other effects, to escape casual notice. What was the purpose? If he wished to murder anyone, be it his wife, or the woman with whom his wife shared house for a time and with whom she formed a friendship during 1963, a pistol was the necessary weapon. One can throw a pistol in a river, or otherwise jettison it, a good deal more easily than a rifle with telescopic sights.''

"You are right, Holmes. The purchase of the rifle presents a puzzle. But you mention that he bought it in March. In that case there was no prior connection with the visit of the President to Dallas in November 1963.''

"Agreed, Watson. We are limiting ourselves to the two questions of why he purchased a high-powered rifle, and why he did so under an assumed name. But if we come nearer to the date of the President's visit, there is the puzzling fact that on or about November 9, 1963, an "Oswald" looked at a car in a showroom and told a salesman that although he could not purchase the vehicle at that time, he had some money coming in—to use Oswald's words, 'in two or three weeks' time.' That was a puzzling statement from a man employed in an unskilled warehouse job at the Texas School Book Depository. Oswald had no other form of income or employment. In American parlance, Oswald did not have a bean. Of course, he could easily have invented the story,

—51

in order to conceal his inability to purchase the car on the spot. But it would have been much easier for Oswald to conjure the more familiar excuse used by a potential customer to avoid or to defer a purchase—that he wished to look at other models on the market, or merely to think it over. To assert that he had some money coming in, very shortly, was an open invitation to the salesman to offer some special terms—a modest deposit, perhaps, or a follow-up, indeed, anything to clinch a purchase in the intensely competitive business of car salesmanship. Salesmen are trained to take careful note of a customer's financial prospects. Why did Oswald make such an unusual excuse on that occasion? Was it his subconscious that prompted the boast about money to a car salesman? Was he drawing attention, obliquely, to a projected plan of which he was a part? Oswald's curious statement has the ring of conviction by its very oddity. The evidence for the statement is well attested in the Volumes of Evidence annexed to the Warren Commission Report."

"Are there further items in your list, Holmes?"

"Quite a few, Watson. But I have time for only one more. We must be off on our journey through the suburbs shortly. When Oswald was arrested and then later charged by Captain Fritz of the Dallas police at 5:30 P.M. on the day of the assassination, he made a curious remark concerning Mrs. Paine, the lady with whom Oswald's wife was lodging. A witness had already asserted that a lady had given Oswald a lift in a station wagon in the vicinity of the School Depository earlier that day. The car was said to resemble Mrs. Paine's car. Oswald's remark to Captain Fritz, in the presence of other police and Secret Service witnesses, went thus. 'Don't try to tie her in to this. She had nothing to do with it. Everybody will know who I am now.' It is this last remark that puzzles me, Watson. We will no doubt return to it in the next few days. What exactly did Oswald mean when he said 'Everybody will know who I am now'?"

6

In many years of association with Sherlock Holmes I had learned to adapt myself to the unexpected and, on occasion, as I observed earlier, to the noxious. If the trail led to some opium den in Hong Kong, or to a seamen's bar on the quayside at Marseilles, or to sinks of iniquity in north African ports, thither would I accompany the master sleuth, knowing that this human bloodhound followed the scent wherever it might lead. Our peregrinations on this afternoon in Dallas in no way matched the noisome haunts of the criminal elements as we had experienced them in sundry towns of Europe and Africa, but it was nonetheless an experience I would not care to repeat.

With his notebook at the ready, Holmes began our odyssey at the Texas School Book Depository, whence we walked some little distance in order to take a bus, and then another bus. At times Holmes consulted a detailed street map on which he had inscribed some curious hieroglyphs. The drab, suburban streets where we walked, the nondescript rooming houses, the grimy shops and liquor stores, the interminable street corner garages assaulting the eye, all contributed a *mise-en-scène* I would have preferred to forego. A silent air of menace, even of brutality, seemed to lie beneath the surface of things. But it was not for me to question my companion's search for possible suggestive leads. In my memory I recalled the Liverpool Ferry Case, and Holmes's sudden perception as we crossed the grubby reaches of the Mersey for the sixth time. It brought the case to a sudden and triumphant conclusion. However, Holmes had warned me often enough since our arrival that there would be no firm conclusions to the present case. I wondered.

We returned to the center of Dallas. Holmes glanced at his chronometer and then treated me to another surprise.

"I think that is our limousine over there," he observed. Across the street I saw a car of ample proportions, with tinted windows at the rear that made it impossible to penetrate the interior of the conveyance.

As we came to the car, our driver of the previous day emerged from the front seat and held open the rear door.

"Good afternoon, sir," he said. Holmes inclined his head in a greeting and together we settled into the deep upholstered interior. A thick glass screen before us shielded our conversation. I inquired of Holmes our destination.

"The suburb of Irving, where Oswald spent the night before the assassination with his wife, at the home of Mrs. Ruth Paine."

"Do you plan to visit the house?"

"I do not, apart from a discreet inspection. I wish to experience the ambience. I fear I will be detaching myself from your good company once more, Watson. Two English-looking gentlemen will be altogether too conspicuous in the suburban milieu where we are bound."

Our journey took us by way of broad twin highways thrusting their concrete way through a depressing landscape, littered with the detritus of the more unbeautiful aspects of American civilization. The car stopped eventually in a distant suburb, at a street corner where a sign on the lamp post declared WEST 5th ST.. Holmes got out, and gave the driver some instructions, pointing ahead. I remained ensconced. We drew away and, looking behind, I observed Holmes assuming an insouciant, languid pace that only a close confidant would recognize as a ruse to give passers-by the impression of an elderly gentleman taking an afternoon constitutional. I well knew that Holmes's mind was never so alert and attuned as on these peripatetic occasions. Every sight and sound of the scene would be absorbed into his mind for any nuance they might convey. Holmes was learning for himself what it might be like to live in these characterless surroundings. I therefore contained my impatience, and fell into a slight doze as we waited for him by the curbside, some ten or twelve blocks further along this tedious thoroughfare.

The reconnoiter took about half an hour. As we drove back to Dallas, I wondered if Holmes had reached some minor, tentative conclusion as he soliloquized.

"Watson, I fear those mean surroundings provide a motive of sorts for a man to kill a rich and successful President with a beautiful wife. Oswald was dispossessed of everything: of wealth, education, public recognition, of any secure family life, of the dazzle of the metropolis —above all, perhaps, he was devoid of power: the awesome power vested by the American Constitution in one man. Oswald was a man of mean temperament, of thwarted ambition, of no certain future, with his marriage in ruins. He was thus, indubitably, a potential assassin of a rich and powerful President."

"You begin to share the conclusions of the official Report, then?" I began.

"Not yet. I am merely adopting part of its train of thought. There are recalcitrant elements in the hypothesis of the lonely young man plotting the death of the President entirely unaided, sharing his dread secret with no one, uncertain above all else that he will succeed. Even the psychopath can require someone to whom he can divulge his design, in order to measure, or at the least to gain some purchase on the scheme, especially one of such enormity. As I observed earlier, Oswald did not possess the madness of the true psychopath. Violent tendencies, yes, as many men in this city and this state possess, through its peculiar addiction to the law of the gun. But not the dementia so often present in the clinical condition, as you must know from your professional experience, Watson."

Holmes was correct. From the details of the case I had studied, I agreed that medical opinion could not have adjudged Oswald a psychopath. However, I reminded Holmes of the detailed account of that final night before the assassination, provided in the book by Mr. William Manchester under the title *Death of a President.* I had taken time to study the book, which Holmes had passed to me, since it was much the most detailed narrative extant of all the events surrounding that day of infamy, and the author had been at pains to check the movements of the principal characters in the finest detail.

"Let us recall, Holmes," I began, "that on the night before the assassination, Oswald's marriage collapsed, that he was deeply humiliated in the house his wife shared with Mrs. Paine, and that, in Mr. Manchester's view, he quietly went mad as he watched the television screen.''

"I recall the narrative and the author's words, which you relate with complete fidelity," Holmes put in. "It is one of the few points in that impressive account where I would question the author's assertions. The chief witness for what occurred in Mrs. Ruth Paine's household that evening was Oswald's wife, Marina Oswald. Mrs. Paine's testimony is supportive. But one would hardly single out those witnesses as the most detached among the many who gave evidence on different aspects of the events before and after the assassination. The relationship between the two ladies was complex. They had implicitly agreed to exclude Oswald from their association. They were bound together in friendship, emotionally though not sexually, if I may be candid. It could well be that when Marina Oswald refused her husband's entreaties that evening for the rehabilitation of their marriage —if such entreaties occurred—Oswald sat before the television screen and ceased to be *compos mentis.* And as you observe, Watson, Mr. Manchester indeed asserts—I recall the precise statement—that Oswald was not really watching the flickering screen, but that he was going mad and that this particular form of madness does not strike suddenly—it had been in process for all of Oswald's life.

"But we must ask what evidence the author had for these interpretations. None that would stand up in a court of law, I fear. They are mere conjecture. But there is a greater difficulty. If the foul deed was finally sparked by Oswald's humiliation before these two women in Irving that same evening, it fails to explain his methodical construction of a paper container at the Book Depository earlier that day, or perhaps earlier that week, in order to conceal the weapon he intended—and had planned—to collect from the garage of the house in Irving on this particular evening. The plan, and the intention, were clearly present some time before Oswald met his wife that evening. Our question is: how much earlier was the plan conceived? As my French colleagues in the *Deuxième Bureau* would put it, the question imposes itself."

We had arrived back at the center of Dallas. The traffic had thickened in the canyonlike streets where office blocks raised their many stories to blot out the late afternoon sunshine filtering across the pale sky above. The driver had clearly been given detailed instructions and, after two further turns at busy street corners, I saw before us the gentle incline of the road moving down toward the underpass at Dealey Plaza. The driver dropped his speed to a very slow cruise, of no more than ten miles per hour, on the center lane of the highway. As we moved down and passed the grassy knoll toward the underpass, I could not prevent a strange chilling sensation. Although, as a medical practitioner, I am professionally well used to those moments where life departs from a person, so that the living being is replaced by the cadaver, sometimes in distressing circumstances, I confess that on this occasion, I experienced the strange and unwonted sensation of the hair rising at my collar. I instinctively settled myself somewhat lower in the interior of the limousine. Happily, the eerie moment passed within seconds.

With Holmes, it was different. He swivelled about to glance through the rear window of the car, and I could see that his vision was trained aloft, and to the left rear. As quickly did he swing about and lean forward, glancing to the right now, then forward again, as we came to the underpass. The car then speeded up, as the irate faces of drivers showed behind and about us, and they sounded their horns shrilly. Again, one felt the tensions of this city. It was an immense relief when the car finally brought us back to the front of our hotel and the driver departed with a brief salute, as courteously and as discreetly as could be wished.

We ascended to our suite in the lift. I observed that Holmes was deep in thought, so I went to my bedroom, drew a bath, disrobed, and allowed the hot water to enfold me for some fifteen minutes or more. At some level of the subconscious I had experienced a sense of contamination during the afternoon, and I now recognized in myself the symptoms known to colleagues in psychological medicine—a cleansing ritual.

I dressed, then rejoined Holmes in our sitting room. He was writing at the small table by the window, enveloped by the fumes of his pipe. I observed his favorite Grosvenor mixture in the aromatic air.

"Ah, there you are, Watson," he exclaimed, as he flung down his pen. "I may be extending our itinerary somewhat."

"Whither, and when?" I asked. My features no doubt registered alarm and chagrin.

"To other cities," said Holmes enigmatically. "I must also examine some more documents and materials at the National Archives in Washington. We may be there for three days. I may have some calls *en route*, and if I fail to inform you of them, Watson, you must accept that I am the recipient of some special confidences from our clients that I am not at liberty to divulge, not even to you, my good friend."

Once again, I made no demur. I recalled the Monaco Jewels Case, almost two decades earlier, when Holmes was admitted to some of the most intimate secrets of the private lives of European nobility as he traced the culprit's ingenious exploitation of human weaknesses. The present case was quite different in its context and much more important in its significance, but I readily acknowledged that there might be good reasons for a degree of furtiveness on Holmes's part. However, my curiosity was stirred by the closely written notes on the table.

"Are you following any particular line of reasoning, Holmes?" I ventured to ask.

"You will recall, Watson, that in the Thor Bridge Case, I reminded you that where a crime is premeditated, then the means of escaping from the scene of the crime must also be premeditated. There is an important corollary to that point which I confess came to me only this afternoon during our drive back from Irving. If there is a successful assassination and then a rapid getaway from the crime, as occurred in this case, it must either be explained by astounding luck, or by careful planning. We have already noted that at Oswald's place of work that morning, for a vital half hour or more, first awaiting the President— with due allowance for possible delays to the motorcade —and then immediately after, when shots rang out from an upper window (the shots very audible throughout the interior of the School Book Depository), not one of Oswald's fellow workers, or the Superintendent, or anyone inside the building or immediately outside observed Oswald at the scene of the crime before it occurred. However, he was found in the lunch room on the second floor, perfectly calm, minutes later. There are a number of very puzzling aspects to this. Oswald was deeply interested in the personalities of politics. He would know, quite certainly, that the President, his wife, and an entourage would be passing just outside his workplace during that lunch hour. Would he not wish to be there, to witness the motorcade? Would not simple curiosity have impelled him? Why, then, do we find him ignoring what all his fellow workers were witnessing? Did he see the motorcade? If so, where? If not, why not? Was he otherwise occupied? But if he was occupied in the assassin's act, in full view of hundreds of onlookers and scores of his fellow workers immediately beneath the window where he committed the deed, why then did he tarry at a vending machine in the lunch room of the Depository, instead of making a quick getaway by way of the rear entrances, only one short flight of stairs beneath? Why? I confess that I can find no clear or satisfactory answer to this puzzle at this stage.

"I am reluctant to conclude that Oswald was insane. It was more likely that he was in a remarkably cool—even a very collected state of mind. Certainly, it requires a very cool head to fire off at least three shots, aimed with a steady hand, a calm eye, and deadly accuracy, in very rapid succession. In all its details, before and after the crime, the timing was perfect. Yet a madman, acting alone, his matrimonial affairs in shreds after an altercation with his wife the previous night, was not likely to plan and then put into effect in a matter of hours a highly skilled operation showing a mastery of timing and great attention to detail. It is possible, but it is not probable."

"You are therefore rejecting the theory that Oswald acted alone and killed the President without accomplices to the act?"

"I am not rejecting it, Watson. Neither am I accepting

it. At present, I am trying to reconstruct the crime, and much the most vital part of that reconstruction is the state of mind of Lee Harvey Oswald at the time of the President's death. Unless we know more about that—whether we proceed by logical analysis, by deduction, or by putting two and three and five together, we will not get far. There are aspects of the official Report and its explanation of events that I find altogether too neat. It is all too cut and dried. Others have made the point—and I concur—that the Warren Commission reads more like a prosecuting counsel's brief against an accused individual than a search for truth. The more recent documents and Hearings of the Congressional Committee on the Assassination are not different in kind."

"But, as you remind me, Holmes, there are the twenty-six volumes of evidence, of which the Report is itself only a digest, and the Congressional hearings were very meticulous," I remonstrated. I knew that Holmes liked me to put the opposing case on occasion, if only to stretch his mind.

"Agreed, my dear Watson. But do not be overawed by the sheer bulk of those volumes. A good many pages are taken up with testimony that is either irrelevant or useless. There are a great many exhibits covering many pages. One of the exhibits is the contract Marina Oswald signed for publication rights of her story within two weeks of the assassination. Yet Mrs. Oswald was not called to testify to the Warren Commission until February 3, 1964—that is, more than two months after the Commission was set up. It would be surprising if she had not felt the tug of poetic license by then, however slight, since her appetite in pecuniary matters was well established. Mrs. Oswald's evidence was crucial to the final verdict, and indeed forms almost a tenth of the testimony admitted to the Report. Yet she was never cross-examined as a witness, and she changed her testimony between February and September 1964 in certain details."

"What details, pray?"

"Several, but one that interested me considerably was her assertion in September 1964 that she always thought her husband was aiming at Governor Connally in the President's open car, and not at the President. A curious, yet crucial emendation, if there were any substance to it."

"Adornment to the earlier tale, possibly. You mentioned her desire for lucre."

"Possibly. But curious, none the less. Ten months after her husband's death, when his presence and his spirit could no longer trouble her, it is possible that remorse of some kind or other may have struck. Oswald was, after all, the father of Marina Oswald's two children. And yet, a pathetic figure of a man, domestically. He could not cope with the challenge to his manhood presented by two powerful women. Marina Oswald could have been moved by pity. Ten months after her husband's death, she may well have been moved to render him some form of homage, however slight, by speaking plainly, perhaps more accurately."

"But what do you make of the extraordinary suggestion—that Oswald was firing at Governor Connally?"

"It is not impossible. Oswald could have been hired for such a purpose. A deep feud divided the Democratic Party in Texas at the time. It dominated all the news. It was featured in the newspapers Oswald was reading. Connally belonged with the right-wing faction, the bankers, the rich men of Dallas. A natural enemy, for one of

Oswald's persuasion. Governor Connally had risen from extreme poverty by ferociously clawing his way upward, beating down his political enemies. He finally achieved power and wealth. It was commonly asserted that the Governor felt comfortable only in expensive, hand-tailored suits and custom-made shoes. He was undoubtedly an object of deep resentment and consuming envy to men like Oswald, also born to poverty, but destined to remain there. Moreover, Oswald had a deep personal resentment against Governor Connally, since it was he, in an earlier role as Secretary of the Navy, who signed Oswald's dishonorable discharge from the Marines on account of his defection to the Soviet Union. This rankled with Oswald, who sought to have it rescinded, always without success."

"But in that case, Holmes, what could have induced Oswald to switch his target to the President?"

"He may not have done. He may have been hired to shoot at Connally. Connally was shot. The bullet wounding Connally was held to be the same bullet that passed through the President's neck. But expert witnesses denied this at the time. Aside from that, Oswald could quite easily have missed his aim at a small, moving target."

"But there was expert medical evidence on that point, was there not?"

"The entry and exit wounds at the President's throat were the most hotly disputed aspect of the medical evidence adduced at the autopsy on the President. Urgent surgery was attempted on the President in Dallas as his life ebbed away—including a tracheotomy at the front of his throat. More than one physician has asserted that the bullet that hit the President in the neck could not have hit Governor Connally in its downward trajectory. There is abundant testimony that three shots at the very least were fired in Dealey Plaza on the day of the killing. Some witnesses suggested four shots, some five, but these sounds could have been due to the echo effects about the plaza. Ballistics experts later asserted that Oswald could not have fired three shots within five seconds with the weapon found in the Book Depository. Hence the two shot, single assassin theory, though of course two shots do not testify to a single assassin, nor to a single weapon. They could equally point to two assassins, if there is no conclusive proof linking two bullets to one gun. If more than one person was implicated in the murder of the President, a number of factors would point to two assassins."

"Pray elucidate, Holmes."

"There was the problem of who would have the frightful task of pressing the trigger. Which of the accomplices would be ready to assume that burden without assistance, alone among the conspirators? Would he not insist on an accomplice for the deed at the very least—if only to ensure against failure in case his aim was unsteady at the crucial moment? Two marksmen must always be better than one, for such an unsavory task."

"What, then, do you envisage as a possible explanation of the crime?"

"There is no one explanation that fits the available facts more neatly than any other—still less one that excludes other explanations. Oswald could have been involved as an accomplice to marksmen aiming at Governor Connally. A political shot across the bows, for a price, from who knows which elements in this violent society? Oswald may have thought this was his mission up to and including the fatal moment when the President, and not Connally, became the chief victim. If so, Oswald was the victim of an ingenious "frame-up," in American parlance. If he observed the effects of the shots, it would have taken him only a matter of seconds to grasp the enormity of the crime in which he was now inextricably involved. But he may not have observed the shots if he was merely an accomplice."

"And what is your belief, Holmes?"

"I do not know, Watson. I confess I do not know, and I am still far short of even an inference on probabilities. There is such a confusion of testimony. Recall Governor Connally's shouts, as witnesses in the car later testified. The President had already been hit. Then Governor Connally felt the bullet in his side. He shrieked, "No, no, no! They're going to kill us both!" I have pondered the phrases of that sudden reaction. We must allow that the Governor was in a state of complete shock, terrified for his life, likely to shout anything. Instinct must have prompted him to assume more than one assassin as the bullets found their mark. So it would have seemed, most certainly, if shots had come from the front, as well as from the rear. If lone shots had come from the rear only, one at a time, it is possible that the Governor might instinctively have conjectured the lone assassin, for that has been the rule in history when American Presidents fell before the assassin. But in this case, Governor Connally instinctively selected the plural. That is what I mean, Watson, when I refer to unconsidered trifles in this case, as in other cases we have worked on together. Here, there may be some significance, or there may not be. I do not know."

I gazed at Holmes, silenced by what now seemed to be the import of his speculations.

"You believe, Holmes, that Oswald was not a lone assassin? That there was a conspiracy to murder the President?"

Holmes sprang from his chair and walked to the open window. Dusk had advanced to darkness and the neon lights of the city glinted into the room. He did not answer immediately, but when he did, I knew that his thoughts had moved on since we left the hotel that morning; that one or two pieces of the vast jigsaw may have begun to form a tiny pattern on the discordant canvas presented to that acute mind.

"Watson," he said slowly, "I say only that I believe that neither the official investigation and the Warren Report that followed it, nor the recent Congressional hearings have arrived at the whole truth. Elements of the truth, most certainly, many of them pertinent. But the whole truth? I think not. These are deep waters, Watson. Deep, and decidedly muddy. We will discuss them after we have dined. Let us put our minds to other things meanwhile."

7

During dinner we discussed my own plans to hand over my medical practice to my junior partner at the end of the year. I felt I had had a good innings, and my wife's visits to the West Country had finally resulted in the location of a handsome stone-built house in Dorset. I was looking forward to quitting the hurly-burly of the metropolis to take up rural pursuits—fishing, perhaps a dabble at the painter's art—above all, to a time free of the constant demands of the practice.

When dinner had been cleared away, we sat with a whiskey. Holmes went to his room and brought back the now familiar volume of the official Report on the President's assassination, the deep blue cover stamped with the golden seal and the imperial eagle clutching the symbols of peace and war. '*E Pluribus Unum*': I recalled the motto above the eagle's head, and the tragic irony of the Report's contents struck me forcefully. Holmes was leafing through the volume, with a forest of paper slips, many of them dog-eared, between the pages.

"Let us hypothesize, Watson," he remarked at last. "You are planning to kill the most closely guarded person in the world. Four needs present themselves above all others if you are to accomplish this dastardly mission. What are they?"

I pondered the question carefully. Only three answers came to me.

"A concealed position. Deadly accuracy of aim. An ideal line of fire."

"And the fourth?"

I paused.

"Think, Watson, think through your plan."

"But of course," I added, as the obvious truth dawned quickly. "An effective, rapid means of escape."

"Correct," Holmes pronounced. "We are reducing the problem to its bare essentials. Now tell me, Watson, could Lee Harvey Oswald be expected to secure all four of those vital necessities from a lonely perch, six floors above a crowded plaza, with a thousand onlookers, an open door at the front of the building, his fellow workers gathered there, and—for all he knew—moving about on other floors beneath him? Perhaps on the same floor? There was no knowing in advance. Then an awkward trajectory, downward at an angle of some 20 to 25 degrees, on a small moving target, the line of fire partly obstructed by branches, with two to three shots available at the very most. How say you, Watson, what sort of person would commit himself as a solitary assassin to such an attempt?"

"Only a madman, surely. Most assuredly, he could not have foretold an empty sixth floor, a free field of fire, still less an easy escape. And Oswald was not mad."

"Indeed he was not. During several interrogations that weekend, he was explicitly cognizant of his legal rights —and he even discoursed on the several different methods of interrogation which, he said—and we should note this carefully—he knew the FBI was wont to employ."

I could not fathom the point Holmes seemed to be indicating, but I assented to his main argument: that Oswald had shown himself to be cogent after several gruelling interrogations. If he could carry his faculties through such an ordeal, subjected to intense questioning by nameless officials in the hubbub of the Dallas police station through two nights and two days, he was not mad. On the contrary, his mental alertness, his reasoning powers and his resilience seemed somewhat above the ordinary. My reverie was interrupted.

"It follows indubitably, Watson. Either this collected and calculating man was, before the deed, ready and willing to be caught red-handed, or he had assistance that gave some assurance of seclusion for the vital period, and a line of escape. It is clear that Oswald was not willing to be caught red-handed. On the contrary, his efforts to elude pursuit and capture extended—according to the official Report—from darting in and out of taxi cabs to shooting a police officer, to taking refuge in a cinema without paying for his ticket. These were the actions of a man attempting to elude capture at all costs . . . of a man who was certainly not seeking martyrdom. They are also, however, the actions of a man who was suddenly confused—indeed in a state of panic, which contrasts markedly with the cool and collected behavior before and immediately after the killing. What does this suggest to you, Watson?"

I wracked my brains but could not quite catch the drift of Holmes's thinking.

"Tell me, Holmes."

"They suggest, Watson, the actions of a man whose plan has miscarried—suddenly and unexpectedly; a man

—71

taken by surprise, in a state of shock, not ready to flee the city—he had no funds for this in any case. But possibly of a man who needed an hour or two of respite for events to become clearer."

"You are clearly proposing, Holmes, that Oswald may have been a party to a plot, but who suddenly discovered that he had been duped?"

"That is one possibility. There are others. Have they occurred to you?"

I shook my head. Perhaps the whiskey had slowed my thinking. Not so, Holmes. The familiar gleam was in his eyes.

"It is possible that Oswald himself was merely the accomplice: the man who arranged the getaway for the assassin. Consider. Ten minutes after the assassination, the Report tells us—here, on page 251—Deputy Sheriff Craig, of Dallas County, interviewed a Mr. and Mrs. Rowland who were onlookers. Mr. Rowland said that he had observed two men on the sixth floor shortly before the assassination, one of whom vanished minutes before the shots rang out. Mrs. Rowland confirmed that her husband had drawn her attention to the two men, although she was looking about at the time, and when her own eyes came to the window, she did not see them. The Report is at pains to discount Mr. Rowland's testimony, on the strength of his wife's statement that she did not witness the two men. It is not often that investigating lawyers select the testimony of a spouse, looking all about her, in an understandable manner, in order to demolish the testimony of an alert and concerned husband. A court of law would make short shrift of such a practice."

"You mentioned other witnesses, Holmes."

"Inside the book depository, two witnesses met Oswald on the second floor minutes after the assassination. The witnesses were a police patrolman and the Superintendent of the building. They were strangers to each other, the policeman drawn to the building by his observation of fire from an upper window. Their movements are given in detail in the Report. They went to the two elevators at the rear of the building, but both cars were on upper floors. The call button did not operate—indicating that the elevator doors were open on some upper floor. The Superintendent called up the elevator shafts twice, 'Turn loose the elevator'—but since neither arrived, he and the policeman ran up the stairs, where they encountered Oswald, only one flight up, on the next floor, sauntering in the lunch room, about to buy himself a soft drink at the vending machine there. The Superintendent of course recognized Oswald as an employee on the workforce. The policeman testified later that Oswald seemed perfectly calm, and not out of breath. Since the simulated time lapse from the shots up to the moment the two witnesses entered the lunch room was put at less than one and a half minutes, this barely gave Oswald time to fire three shots, then descend several flights of stairs in order to stroll to a vending machine, cool, collected, and not out of breath."

"It is possible he assisted the escape of an accomplice?" I queried.

"I believe this to be a reasonable surmise—as reasonable as the existing explanation. If Oswald had shot the President, would he not have taken immediate steps to get out of the building at the rear—where there are several exits? He could then easily have joined the melee that he must surely have expected within seconds of firing through an open window above the head of watching crowds. Why did he not do so? Why did he dally at the lunch room, knowing that he was bound to be held for questioning?"

"It may have been his intention to leave the building, but he may have heard steps coming up the stairs of the building as he descended, so he darted into the lunch room."

"It is possible, Watson. But with a policeman's gun touching the middle portion of his waist—according to the Superintendent's testimony—within two minutes of killing a President, one might have expected some emotion. There was none that either witness could observe. Did Oswald feel that he himself was 'in the clear,' in the American phrase? Or was he simply a cold-blooded assassin?"

"Both seem plausible, Holmes."

"Note, also, the position of the elevators—both of them slow-moving, as I observed for myself, and as the Report confirms. The two witnesses found no elevators on the second, third, or fourth floors as they ascended. At the fifth floor—immediately beneath the assassin's lair—they found one elevator. The other was elsewhere, but the Report is confusing. It suggests that another employee, a Mr. Dougherty, took an elevator down to the ground floor from some upper floor after hearing the shooting, in order to see what was going on outside. Yet our two earlier witnesses—one of them the Superintendent of the building—stated that there was no elevator on the ground floor as they ran upstairs."

"You are suggesting that Oswald, or his accomplices, may have used one of the two elevators?"

"I think not. The plan could not possibly have relied on either of them. There would be uncertainty, first of all, as to their location at the vital period, when every second was crucial. Uncertainty, again, as to who might be encountered in any elevator that happened to be free. No, we must put that means of escape out of our mind, Watson. No one—not even the meanest intelligence—would have planned an escape by means of those ponderous freight elevators. The plan would rest on that ancient but reliable mode of escape—fleetness of foot and hard stairs, whilst ensuring that the elevator was not immediately available on the ground floor for any unexpected ascent."

"But you have already indicated that within minutes the police were bounding up the stairs."

"Long enough for a killer to escape from the rear of the building. But there are more stairs—at the front of the building—close to where the shots were fired, connecting the front vestibule to the second floor, and thus to the rear stairs leading up to the sixth floor."

Holmes held out the Report and indicated the plan of the building. There were indeed stairs at the front of the building, at the southeast corner, leading directly down to the main vestibule at the entrance to the building. I observed that these stairs were separated from the Superintendent's office inside the main ground floor by a wall, with swing doors admitting to an inner vestibule. From the bottom of these stairs, it was but three or four steps to the main street outside. I also noted an elevator in the front vestibule, and it was as if Holmes divined my thoughts.

"No, Watson, the assassin would not have used that elevator either. The same points apply. He would not have relied on it, and who might he not meet if the call button had stopped it on the way up, or the way down?

—75

We come back to the stairs. The front and rear stairs. An assassin would leave by one of those routes, we may be sure. The rear stairs, indeed the whole of the rear of the building, makes for easy egress. Observe the several exits, on each side of the loading docks, leading to the rail yards and to streets north of the Depository. A rear exit would permit an assassin to leave the scene quickly before Dealey Plaza was sealed off by the police."

"How did the assassin get away from the area of Dealey Plaza?"

"Recall, Watson, the testimony of one of the most interesting witnesses to come before the Commission, Mr. Lee Bowers, the railroad towerman on duty in his 14-foot tower well above the railroad yards and the underpass to the rear of the Book Depository. He testified that after traffic had been cut off from the area by the police at mid-morning, he observed three cars enter the area behind the Book Depository and above the underpass where the President's car was due to pass in less than two hours. He described each of the three cars in considerable detail, because they excited his attention by the curious way in which the windows were covered with some kind of red mud. Unusual testimony of this type has the ring of truth: who would choose to daub his car windows with red mud? But from a distance, red cardboard may appear as red mud. Two of the cars had out-of-state license plates, and car stickers indicating they favored a conservative candidate for the Presidency in 1964. According to Mr. Bowers, testifying to the Commission, the first car was driven by a man who appeared to have a microphone held at his mouth. The third car stopped, according to Mr. Bowers, at a point immediately above the grassy knoll at the assassination site."

"Your surmise, Holmes, is that the assassin might have escaped by way of a car parked in that area by prior arrangement?"

"It is possible, Watson. It is possible. There is certainly a singular difficulty in the thesis of the lone assassin, acting without assistance of any kind. Unless we return to the thesis of the martyr. But we have rejected that thesis, as we have also rejected the thesis that Oswald's mind was deranged."

"Can we be certain of that, Holmes?"

"Oswald was a shrewd person, of above average intelligence. He studied and learned to speak Russian. The books he borrowed from a New Orleans public library during his sojourn there—works on history, on philosophy, the novels of Aldous Huxley—not penny crime thrillers—confirm that here was an intelligent person, despite his very limited capacities of self-expression in English prose. What does that entail? It entails that he was more than capable of thinking beyond the act of gunning down a President from the Book Depository where he worked. He would think of the massive manhunt that would bear down instantly on every employee, indeed on every traceable living person who had entered that building for perhaps a decade or more; any person who might know anything of its architectural details, the location of stairs and elevators. On whom would the finger of suspicion first fall? Indubitably on him—a recently hired employee who had defected to Russia, declared himself a Communist, who had married a Russian, who came back to America to defend Cuban independence from the designs of the American political right. The prime suspect, in short, was bound to be Oswald himself.

"So Lee Oswald was either a willing martyr, or he was nothing. He was not a martyr because he protested his innocence—loudly, almost hysterically—during identification parades and police lineups, right to the end. Not a martyr, therefore, unless he had suffered some astonishing and inexplicable change of mind at the moment he fired any shots. In that case, he would not have gone to the second floor lunch room, awaiting the police cordon around the building. And even if he was surprised at that point, his desire, indeed his urgent need to flee the city at once would hardly have taken him to his rooming house half an hour later in a city where every available policeman, every radio patrol car, was on full alert. He would have vanished instantly, swallowed up in another corner of the city, perhaps at the railroad station, or a bus depot, attempting to get away—anywhere but at his place of lodging or the suburb where neighbors, shopkeepers, local garage mechanics, could recognize him. No, Watson, the problem is complex, and yet perhaps elementary. Perhaps Oswald did not expect to be apprehended, convinced by foreknowledge that he would not be charged with the assassination."

"But that *must* mean a conspiracy, Holmes," I exclaimed. "A conspiracy to murder the President of the United States."

"We are not there yet, Watson. One step at a time. The hour is late. We must retire. Here, take this as bedtime reading. I would like your views tomorrow morning on a particular point."

Holmes handed me the heavy volume of the official Report.

"What is it you wish me to study, Holmes?" I asked, weighing the book in my hand.

"Ask yourself if any shots were fired at the President's car from the front, as it moved toward the underpass on Elm Street. Good night, Watson."

With that, Holmes vanished to his room.

8

Holmes brought up the topic as we settled to our breakfast.

"Now, Watson, what did you make of the little problem I set you?"

"I see that members of the Commission addressed themselves to the very speculation you raised, Holmes," I replied.

"Ah yes. The section on 'Speculations and Rumors.' Appendix Number 12, if I remember right." Holmes was indubitably correct.

"The Commission considers the speculation of shots from the front and dismisses it," I observed. "Two policemen and thirteen railroad employees testified that no shots were fired from the rail bridge above the underpass."

"And is that now your view?"

"I think I am bound to accept it, Holmes. I was not there, but . . ."

Holmes held up his hand. "I agree with you. I do not think that any shots were fired from the rail overpass."

"But then why your question, Holmes?"

"I wanted to see if you noticed a lacuna in the list of speculations by the Commission."

"No omissions that come to my mind immediately."

"The Commission concentrated exclusively on the speculation that shots came from the overpass. The photographic exhibits concerning shots from the front also concentrated on that location. But the overpass was an exceedingly improbable hypothesis for a number of reasons. It was overlooked by a great many buildings, including the Book Depository and the railroad tower close by. More than that, many onlookers were scattered along the overpass. An assailant would again need to be a lunatic or a martyr to choose such an overpopulated spot, visible on all sides. If shots were planned from the front, an assassin would need cover—especially overhead cover, as close as possible to the President's car. Pray hand me the Report, Watson."

I reached to the sideboard and handed Holmes the book. He turned the pages rapidly, then passed it back, his slim finger bending over page 33, showing an aerial photograph of Dealey Plaza, with Elm Street curving toward the underpass. Holmes had his finger on the photograph.

"Here, Watson, is the exact spot the President's car had reached when he was shot. Put yourself in the assassin's place if you planned to shoot from the front. Where would you locate yourself?"

"Here," I said, "beneath these trees." I put my finger at the trees immediately above the short grassy knoll descending to the spot where the President was killed.

"Of course you would, Watson. What is more, as we observed ourselves, there are bushes there, also a wooden fence, even a pergola at that spot, although the indistinct photograph hardly shows them from this height. During our walk yesterday morning and on our afternoon drive where you cringed slightly, if you will pardon me, as we passed beneath the overpass, you did not look to your right, to the trees by the grassy knoll. The overpass drew your attention, as it drew the attention of the Secret Service and the police on the fateful day. Indeed, security officers with the President's motorcade gestured to a policeman on the overpass to clear the bridge as the President's car approached. A serious breach of security had occurred. Then came the shots. The acoustics of Dealey Plaza are confusing. Testimony was conflicting, both at the time, and later. Yet a considerable number of the witnesses on the spot said that shots came from somewhere to the front. Others observed shots coming from the Book Depository."

"Which set of witnesses do you believe, Holmes?"

"I am quite ready to believe both."

"Both? So you are suggesting that the assassins doubled their risk of being apprehended by selecting two separate positions instead of a single locality? That hardly seems logical. One well-aimed bullet was all that was required. At least three shots were fired, some say four: more than enough for the deed."

"Watson," my companion interrupted my consternation, as I grappled with the new complications he had now introduced, "which state of the Union are we in?"

"Texas." I was deeply puzzled by this question, which struck me as obtuse.

"And what, traditionally, do you associate with Texas? Think back to your youth, Watson."

"Why, the Wild West. The law of the gun. Taking land from the Indians. Driving cattle."

"Excellent. And can you remember stories, or perhaps visits to the cinema, in which the winning of the West was portrayed. Can you think of the classic technique used in the canyons of the West to lure, and then to kill, with minimum loss to your own side?"

I thought hard for some seconds, but could not catch the drift. I gave up.

"The decoy, Watson. The decoy. The trick is as old as the American Republic, and it was perfected in these states. It is written into the minds of every young man who ever held a gun in these parts. It is part of what we might call their historical subconscious, the way they think. Do you recall the bizarre events at the Dallas police station, when Oswald was shot down by Ruby in the basement? The police were planning to transfer him to another spot. They brought a police car to the basement, but also an armored truck. The truck was—in the words of the police officials at subsequent testimony—a decoy, to lure away the press and television reporters whilst Oswald was to be transferred in a plain police car in another direction."

"You are saying, then, that the lair on the sixth floor of the Book Depository was a decoy to attract attention away from the real assassin close to the President's car?"

"I am saying that this could possibly give us more plausible hypotheses than the official Report supplies or deigns to consider. Even so, any planned decoy did not entirely succeed, and understandably so. Many witnesses, including a policeman, ran up the grassy knoll immediately the shots had stopped. A witness standing on the overpass, Mr. S.M. Holland, testified that he saw a puff of smoke come out from the trees immediately above the grassy knoll, about 6 or 8 feet above the ground. Mr. Holland, let us note, Watson, was the signal supervisor for the Union Terminal Company at the rail yards—he had been at his job for twenty-five years. One could hardly hope for a better on-the-spot witness than a man with keen vision whose employ required him to distinguish signals from the near and middle distance throughout his working career."

"Were there other witnesses, Holmes?"

"There is abundant testimony from other witnesses. In an open car, almost immediately behind the Presidential limousine, Senator Yarborough of Texas caught the smell of gunpowder as the cars swept down Elm Street. So did other witnesses. The odor could hardly have drifted down six stories, across 75 yards, in a matter of two or three seconds."

"But is not this testimony mentioned in the Report?"

"It is, and most briefly. It is discounted, along with that of many other witnesses who declared that they heard shots, or saw a puff, or puffs, of smoke coming from the trees just above the President's car. Indeed, Mr. Holland ran along the overpass to the area of the trees to look for the assassin behind the fence. When he arrived there, he could find only a policeman and plain-clothesmen. His testimony is set out in the Sixth Volume of the Commission's hearings, but alas, his testimony is disregarded in the summary. He—and others who ran there—may have been too late, and of course the attention of the police force was fixed at that moment on the carnage within Dealey Plaza. Nevertheless, a number of men were arrested in the immediate area, and one was kept in jail for several days. He was then released, but his identity has not been disclosed. The local press at first reported that a number of people were held to be implicated in the shooting—a view shared by the Dallas District Attorney, if he was correctly reported on the

—84

front page of the *Dallas Morning News* the morning after the shooting. But after the death of Oswald, all other suspects ceased to exist."

"You appear to suggest, Holmes, that the Dallas police were somehow involved. Is that your suspicion?"

"You use the compendious term 'Dallas police,' Watson. That is much too all-embracing. As you well know, every police force contains at least some—it may be only a handful—who keep strange company for a variety of reasons. For some, it may be the temptations of the flesh; with others, monetary gain is the prize. Others again may have strong views on politics, and on law and order. Policemen are constantly tempted, as you also know, Watson, by those who wish to ensure that the police are on their side; or worse, by those who hope to corrupt them. And this unhappy truth applied in Dallas in 1963, as it applies in London, in Rome, Paris, New York, and Hong Kong. You will recall some of the cases we have worked on together."

I did indeed. Yet I was unable to grasp the connection Holmes seemed to be making.

"Are you suggesting, Holmes, that a Dallas policeman fired at the President?"

"Exceedingly improbable, Watson."

"Why so?"

"A number of reasons. First, the enormity of the crime. Any conspiracy would require the active collaboration of a number of policemen. But note the difficulties for any cabal of policemen—even were they a very small group conspiring together—in plotting to kill a President. They could not know whether, on the precise day, and at the precise time, even behind a fence above a knoll, other colleagues on the force might not see and recognize the man behind the rifle. Who, then, would be willing to be the assassin? Who would risk the certainty of life imprisonment, if not death, and certainly a ruined career, by the chance circumstance of being observed by a colleague, or of some other setback to the plan? Weighing those costs, the man who agreed would also be making himself available for professional suicide—perhaps for capital punishment. Even hatred for a visiting President does not stretch to those limits for any sane individual."

"Do you acquit the police?"

"I do not believe the Dallas police conspired among themselves to kill the President. Even were some of them so inclined, the enormity of the crime would place such a high premium on sealing so many lips among hundreds of patrolmen. The conspirators would not, could not, be so foolish as to risk that."

"What then, Holmes?"

"There is a well-tried institution in the Republic, Watson, as you may know. The hired gunman. The 'hit man,' in the vernacular. These villains exist in most of the big cities. New York and Chicago contain scores of guns for hire. These men do it for money. They are without scruples, without a vestige of morality. If the prize is big enough, they are available. The target dictates the price. There is a great deal of money available in Dallas, I fear. Money would be no problem. The attraction—if that is the word—of the 'hit man' is that he is from out of town. He vanishes as quickly as he appears, once the deed is done, the 'contract' completed. He knows he will get his money, if not on the spot then immediately thereafter, because he knows someone—not necessarily his paymaster, nor even the person who placed the contract. But there is no option but to pay up, or be blackmailed."

"You feel, then, that this was a 'contract'?"

"It is not impossible, Watson."

"But the police were not involved?"

"Not as a plot involving a number of them, as I have observed. The risks posed would far outweigh any possible animosity toward the President. However, there *may* have been those on the Dallas police force who were in touch with the seedier elements of Dallas, the fringes of the underworld where policeman often have contacts in the battle against crime."

"But what was the motive, Holmes? I confess I am baffled. Who would wish to gun down a young President, sitting next to his wife—a cold-blooded murder serving no apparent purpose, bringing a whole nation to grief?"

"You are right to raise the question, Watson. It is indeed the prime question. Remember again that Dallas is something unto itself. Texas is a raw state, proud of its history of conquest and reconquest. Texans consider themselves somewhat apart from other Americans. I took the occasion to immerse myself in the history of the American West before leaving London. I felt this was a necessary prelude to understanding why this appalling tragedy should occur in this state and this city. The starting point must be its history, and then the peculiar nature of Texas politics."

"I confess, Holmes, that medical practice hardly affords me the necessary time to do as you did."

"Of course not, Watson. And indeed, it is not sufficient to stop at the historical retrospect. One must go on to study the peculiar nature of Texas politics, especially in the years—even the months and days—preceding the assassination. It is an unattractive spectacle. So mild a man as Adlai Stevenson was assaulted in this city only four weeks before the assassination. Earlier than that, in 1960, a favorite son of the state, the then Senator Lyndon Johnson and his wife were spat upon because of the liberal nature of their views. If a Texas Senator and his lady could be spat upon, what restraints for the scion of a wealthy, liberal, Catholic family from Massachusetts? I fear I must ask you to leave your gentle ways behind you as you attempt to get into the minds of those we are dealing with, Watson. They did not take your physician's Hippocratic oath. Men are killed in this city almost every day, and as for respecting the law, or authority, policemen are too often the victims themselves of the slayings.

"We must start with Dallas as it is, I fear, and not as we might like it to be. The extremes of the Republic converge here: astounding personal wealth and dire poverty; the worship of God and the worship of Mammon; the polarities of American politics; fervent patriotism and a deep suspicion of alternative political ideas or doctrines. All these combinations are explosive, Watson. If each and all are set against each other in one fell purpose, we can indeed expect the death of a President. That is perhaps why such strange events took place after the assassination—events that would surpass belief in other towns or regions. Most bizarre of all, perhaps, the fact that a person held in custody by the Dallas police, accused of a monstrous crime, surrounded by the officers of the law, within the very bastion of the law enforcement agencies, is then done to death as his guardians look on, careless or unaware, or with unbelievable indifference on the part of many persons at one and the same time. How could this happen, given the historic importance of the crime and of the prime suspect? Nor can we comprehend the bizarre scenes in the office of the Chief of Police when Oswald was interrogated, repeatedly, through two days and two nights."

"More than bizarre, Holmes. Almost beyond comprehension."

"Except in Dallas, Watson. Consider the facts. The President is already dead, so that the enormity of the crime is clear to all, especially to the police officers, the FBI agents, and Secret Service men who are present within the offices of the Chief of Police at Dallas, whilst Oswald is subjected to repeated interrogations. No one, it seemed, throughout that weekend, had a simple recording device in the central headquarters of a busy police station where the recording of testimony by a variety of means is standard procedure, in the interests of due process and of preserving records."

Holmes stopped speaking and lapsed into one of his silences. I detected that he did not wish to be disturbed in his thoughts, so I absented myself to my room and wrote letters to my family at home. A little later I heard Holmes moving about and rejoined him. He seemed to have emerged from his reverie. The quick, light tread of his step indicated that he wanted to be about some business or other.

"Come, Watson. We will take another walk at the scene of the crime. We will go by way of Main Street. I also wish to take a look at the Police Department building."

We put on our coats and soon felt the autumnal crispness in the air as we stepped out of the hotel. Holmes hailed a cab and instructed the driver to go by way of Main Street to Dealey Plaza. At one point Holmes tapped my knee and signalled a building opposite, to our left.

The cab continued to Houston Street and we alighted near the stone balustrades and reflecting pools giving on to Dealey Plaza, which now lay before us. We walked north up Houston Street, crossed once more to that familiar, ugly building; then Holmes turned west, heading along the front of the building to the grassy knoll above Elm Street. He did not speak, but I knew by his measured tread that he was estimating time and distance. I held my peace until he should speak again. To our left was the unsightly pergola, beyond it a fence, with trees above and about it. The short road gave out, and we found ourselves gazing at a car park, then beyond at railroad tracks across our front, with cars parked on either side of broad marshaling yards, close to a short branch line going past the rear of the Texas Book Depository. Looking over the scene, I was struck by the many places available for a getaway car to locate itself behind the Depository, with easy lines of departure to roads and suburbs lying north of Elm Street.

Holmes turned to me as I took in the scene. "Tell me, Watson, what does this lead you to believe?"

"That any assailants in this area would choose this route to escape."

"Correct. The other possibility is that they remained where they were, but even the most cursory knowledge of psychology suggests that they would plan to quit the scene immediately, since they would fear witnesses on the spot."

We returned to the grassy knoll in Dealey Plaza. I entered an objection.

"But if memory serves, Holmes, each of the shots heard by witnesses was accounted for; the trajectories led in a downward path from an upper window of the

Book Depository down and into the President's car."

"There is no doubt whatever that three shots at least came from a high vantage point to the rear of the car, Watson. But as to further shots, and how many precisely, and their trajectory, the evidence is confused. Bear in mind the very curious acoustics of the Plaza—you have no doubt observed them yourself on our visits. At the first shot on that day, pigeons rose in a cloud, swirling about the rooftops. Then another shot, then another. Now apart from the visual testimony of a shot, or shots, from the grassy knoll, let us recall the evidence of a member of the press, Mr. Robert H. Jackson, a staff photographer, if my memory serves me, on the *Dallas Times Herald.* Mr. Jackson was in a car reserved for the gentlemen of the press, some eight or nine cars from the front, and thus located on Houston Street, about halfway between Main Street and Elm Street, away from Dealey Plaza. As we have often had occasion to reflect, Watson, men trained to observe and report events in detail, as a professional calling, make excellent on-the-spot witnesses when events are moving fast. They are much better than the average citizen in first observing and then recalling precisely what occurred, since their livelihood depends on it. Mr. Jackson testified to the Commission that he heard several shots, but that the second and third shots were much closer together than the first and second shots. Many other witnesses gave the same account, quite independently. Some witnesses said that the second and third shots seemed to be instantaneous. Does that suggest anything to you?"

"That the third shot could have come from another weapon."

"Precisely, Watson, if we discount suggestions of

echoes. If there were echoes, Mr. Jackson would have reported four shots at least. Moreover, he was relying solely on his hearing. His eyes were not distracted by the scenes in Dealey Plaza at that moment, since these were not in view. His ears told him that the third shot came much closer to the second than the second did to the first. As you know, there was much argument and debate about the ability to reload a somewhat cumbersome bolt-operated rifle in the time recorded by the frames of the film taken by Mr. Zapruder. Argument ceases if the third shot did not come from the rifle found in the Depository, but from another weapon located elsewhere, which fired immediately after a second shot from the Book Depository, designed to draw attention away from the area to the front of the President's car. It is interesting to note that Mr. Jackson's testimony would seem to be independently confirmed by Mrs. Cabell, the wife of the Mayor of Dallas, riding in a follow-up car closer to the President. Mrs. Cabell stated that when the first shot rang out, she turned to her husband in the car, but at that moment 'the second two shots rang out.' "

"But you forget, Holmes," I interjected, "that if a second weapon was fired from the grassy knoll, the ballistics experts could be expected to find the bullet and contrast the markings with those on the Italian rifle owned by Oswald. The assassins would surely be taking a grave risk?"

"That element of risk is reduced for a highly skilled marksman aiming at the skull of a man in a slow-moving car. Moreover, in the prodigious variety of ammunition available to the assassin in modern times, there is strong appeal in a type of bullet that shatters on impact with any hard structure, such as a human skull. Once shattered, the bullet cannot be traced to the rifling of any particular gun barrel, even though the cartridge case may be traceable to a particular weapon—*if* the cartridge case is found. As you know, the skull is immensely strong, and the top of the President's head was blown off. Recall, Watson, that a large portion of the President's skull was seen to fly off to the rear, and police motorcyclists behind the car were sprayed with his blood. The Zapruder film also shows an upward curving spray of blood traveling to the rear, when the car was moving at no more than ten miles an hour. A bullet from the rear, blowing off the top of the President's head, would have carried the skull with it into the forward portions of the car, and a good deal of blood and tissue along with it. That did not happen. Portions of the skull were retrieved from the street, not from the car."

I nodded, but Holmes could observe my bafflement. What he now suggested could only mean that Oswald—if he was the person firing from the book store—was in league with other persons located on the knoll in some conspiracy. As so often happened, Holmes read my thoughts.

"I know, my dear Watson, that responsible men resist conspiracy theories, and nowhere more readily than when a head of state is done to death, since such a conspiracy would immediately appear as a threat to the very fabric of society itself, as we have already noted and discussed."

"It would help me, Holmes, if you would kindly set out what you feel was the possible sequence of the shots."

"I cannot know for certain, Watson. I am merely supplying a possible explanation for an untidy set of facts. As you know, a considerable number of people stated that they saw, or heard, at least one shot from the knoll. It was a pity so many of them were not called to testify to the Commission. Those who took photographs on the spot and handed them over to the authorities saw their property taken away, perhaps to the National Archives. The Commission, in its Report, concentrates exclusively on the overpass for any alternative theory for shots from the front. That in itself is extraordinary, since hardly a single witness testified to such an unlikely location. The many official photographs of the overpass printed in the Report, and taken from a variety of angles, manage to omit entirely any detail of the knoll, with its trees, its wooden fence, its pergola. The only exception is the distant aerial photograph we examined earlier, taken from the west rather than the east, so that all detail is extremely indistinct, whilst the overpass and railroad tracks dominate the foreground of the photograph. There are also very detailed aerial photographs of areas west of Dealey Plaza, beyond the overpass, that have no relevance to the inquiry other than to show the route to the hospital. It is most curious, but one searches the Report in vain for any photograph of the wooded part of the knoll beyond the pergola above Elm Street, where scores of witnesses asserted they saw, or heard, evidence of at least one shot. Most regrettable."

"But my dear Holmes," I remonstrated, "you are surely not suggesting that the eminent lawyers and politicians recruited from far and near to serve on the Warren Commission—you are not suggesting, surely, that they were part of some elaborate conspiracy?"

"Of course not, Watson." My companion sighed. "I fear it is much more complicated than that. The Commission presented the evidence it had received, but even before it had its first meeting, the theory of the lone assassin, together with a mass of testimony buttressing that theory, had been presented from a limited number of powerful and reputable sources—most notably from the FBI."

"But again, Holmes, you do not suggest that . . ."

"No, I do not, Watson. Large organizations can act in curious ways, sometimes in an aberrant, but that is not to say a guilty fashion. Where their own reputation is at stake—I believe the Americans use the term 'public image'—they can act with a zealous disregard for dispassionate appraisal. Come, it is time to go. We will talk further about these aspects when we have lunched. We will walk by way of the Dallas Police Department on Main Street. I wish to view the ramp where Mr. Jack Ruby strolled, so freely and by such an astonishing and fateful coincidence, at the precise moment when the manacled Lee Harvey Oswald was led from the basement of the Dallas Police Department on the Sunday morning of that murderous weekend."

9

When we regained our hotel, Holmes announced the change of itinerary that he had broached earlier. Instead of returning directly to Washington, where our hosts had placed the residence in Georgetown at our disposal, we were to go to New Orleans. I expressed my surprise.

"You do not have to accompany me, Watson," he observed. "In your place I would choose the attractions of Washington. I fear the visit to New Orleans will entail some inspection of the less attractive quarters of the city."

"You will not expose yourself to danger, Holmes," I cautioned.

"Never fear, my old friend. My incognito will be preserved."

"My choice is to come with you, Holmes."

"Excellent. There is a plane this afternoon. We will be there by evening."

"May I ask the purpose of our visit?"

"I wish to stroll in the vicinity of Lafayette Square, and I have an appointment at the city library."

I did not inquire further. I knew that Holmes would have good reasons for these strange errands. Eventually he might divulge his reasons. But again, he might not. I packed my luggage, and as we sat down to lunch in our suite, the waiter gone, I raised once more the question of the shots in Dealey Plaza.

"I take it, Holmes, that you see a definite complicity linking the shots from the Book Depository and possible shots from the grassy knoll?"

"The possibility of a mere coincidence had occurred to me, Watson, but in fact too many coincidences would have to come together for that to be a reasonable surmise."

"Pray elaborate."

"In the first place, there is the curious fact that Oswald was well known to the Dallas police, to the local branch of the FBI, to the State Department and to the CIA as a defector to Russia, a man of declared Marxist sympathies, with a Russian wife, employed in a building overlooking the President's route. Yet apparently all these agencies were unaware of his whereabouts until minutes after the assassination, when quite suddenly an extraordinary degree of efficiency was shown in locating him at large in the suburbs of Dallas.

"But let us imagine that Oswald was left to his own devices on the fateful morning, and let us further imagine that he planned an attempt on the President's life entirely alone. The film taken by Mr. Zapruder shows the President first reacting to shots coming from the rear. He clutches his neck. If those who planned to shoot from the knoll were quite suddenly presented with unexpected overhead shots from their own flank, is it really likely that in the split seconds intervening they would continue with their plan? Instinct would suggest that any shots coming high from a building immediately beyond the grassy knoll were aimed by the Secret Service at anyone leveling a gun at the President. That same instinct of fear would make any assassin on the knoll crouch in alarm, rather than take careful aim at a moving car in an area crowded with onlookers. No, if the two events were detached and not linked, Watson, any persons on the knoll would have instantly feared for their lives, expecting a fusillade from the scores of men trained to protect the life of the President twenty-four hours a day.

"We come back to the device of the decoy. Oswald, or an accomplice, with an indifferent weapon on the sixth floor, his vision partly obstructed by the branches of a tall oak tree before the building, with a difficult trajectory to a small, moving target—such a hazardous combination could hardly suffice for a vital design. Those involved would need a 'back-up,' and it may indeed have been part of the plan that if Oswald had clearly succeeded in killing the President by the time the limousine emerged from the large roadsign observed in Zapruder's film, then supporting fire from the knoll would not be required. The second part of the ambush could be dispensed with. Oswald may or may not have been privy to that part of the plan. He may have been deluded in any of several different ways that morning, not least in his quick arrest, and then the remorseless interrogation, where he insistently denied any complicity, and demanded a lawyer."

"But Oswald surely expected to be arrested if, as you observe, Holmes, he was already under general suspicion for his political activities?"

"Arrested, perhaps. Publicity, certainly—instant and worldwide. But conviction? Not if he thought he was part of some official plan. That may be one reason why Oswald died too soon. Perhaps he knew too much."

"To what do you refer, Holmes?" I queried, puzzled by this new twist in my friend's reasoning.

"I cannot be sure, Watson. But, as I have observed several times, there are deeply puzzling features to the case against Lee Oswald. You will have noticed the two aliases he adopted."

"Indeed. At his rooming house in Dallas he was 'O. H. Lee,' and at other times 'A. J. Hidell.' "

"It is the second alias that is most interesting for us. He took that name in New Orleans too, and used it for renting private boxes in the post offices for delivery of mail at New Orleans and in Dallas. He also used the name to purchase the rifle said to have killed President Kennedy, as we have already noted, and the pistol held to have killed Police Officer Tippit. It was more than a simple alias, however, because at the time of his arrest, cards bearing official identification of service in the Marines and of Selective Service, each of them forgeries bearing the name Hidell, were on his person."

"What do you conclude from that, Holmes?"

"I place them together with many more associations and pieces of evidence suggesting that Oswald was, in some fashion, in touch with a government agency. As a man who had once defected, then been readmitted to the United States, he was harassed somewhat by local agents of the FBI, both in Dallas and in New Orleans. Oswald might have felt impelled to assume an alias for concealing his whereabouts, but in that case the name O.H. Lee (sometimes he used H. O. Lee) sufficed. To go to the lengths of carrying forged Selective Service and Marine Corps cards on his person, and no other form of identification, all in the name of A. J. Hidell, suggests another category of incognito."

"But you are omitting his active work for the left-wing group supporting Fair Play for Cuba. Indeed his membership card for that group was also on his person in the name of Hidell, if I remember correctly."

"You do so remember, Watson, and I do not forget it. Indeed, the plot thickens with mention of the latter. Oswald was intelligent enough to know that forging Government identification cards was a criminal offense. Putting that offense together with his declared membership in the Fair Play for Cuba Committee—an organization under permanent and active surveillance in Dallas and in New Orleans, the picture becomes even more complicated."

"In what manner?"

"It is a little too early to say. Many pieces of the jigsaw are elusive and puzzling, including some of Oswald's friendships and associations in the Dallas community. There are many examples, but among the more curious was his friendship with an elderly couple, the De Mohrenschildts. The couple knew the Oswalds well—perhaps better than anyone else, other than Marina Oswald's friend Mrs. Ruth Paine, who shared her house with Mrs. Oswald for a time. But regrettably, the De Mohrenschildts' testimony to the Commission was extremely brief. Both had long and exotic careers behind them. Mr. De Mohrenschildt was born in Russia, in the Ukraine, the son of a landowner, and fled with his parents after the Russian Revolution. His wife was born in China, of White Russian parents, and their subsequent careers suggest that they were anything but friendly to any Communist regime, whether in Russia or Cuba. Mr. De Mohrenschildt was in a Polish military academy as a young man, then later studied at Antwerp and Liege, where the university awarded him a doctoral degree in international commerce in 1928. He worked for French intelligence during the war, then became a citizen of the United States in 1949, and was closely involved in oil exploration and production. As a geologist and petroleum engineer, he traveled around the world, and the Commission notes that by a happenstance he was in Guatemala at the time of the Bay of Pigs invasion against Cuba. He and his wife also journeyed to Panama, through the more primitive parts, and wrote a log for the United States Government on what they observed there. The couple were also involved with government-sponsored business ventures in Haiti up to June 1963. They owned a residence there.

"The Dallas community knew the couple as strong and outspoken believers in individual liberties and the American form of government. They hardly seem the ideal couple for an ex-defector, the pro-Castro Lee Harvey Oswald to engage in friendship. It is unfortunate that the testimony of this much traveled and highly intelligent couple is so brief, by contrast to many less articulate witnesses, who testified to the Commission at considerable length. It also seems somewhat superfluous of the Commission to note that no signs of subversive or disloyal conduct had been detected in the De Mohrenschildts; that there was no evidence linking them in any way with the assassination. Perhaps lawyers for the couple insisted on inclusion of the statement, and we must accept it in good faith. But it must strike one as redundant, just as their association with Oswald strikes an odd note.

"George De Mohrenschildt seemed unsure of the occasion when he first met Oswald, but as far as he could remember, he went with a friend, one Colonel Orlov, to Oswald's residence in the slums of Fort Worth, Texas, before Oswald moved to Dallas. A curious pilgrimage for a very successful entrepreneur. Perhaps the association grew from there."

"It would surely repay you, Holmes, to interview this exotic character."

"Impossible, Watson."

"How so?"

"He died, shot to death, apparently by his own hand, at Palm Beach in Florida, in March 1977."

"Was foul play suspected?"

"I do not have the facts. But strange that he shot himself on the second day of a four-day session of interviews he granted to the writer Mr. Edward Jay Epstein, who was at work on a book investigating Oswald's defection to Russia and his possible associations with espionage activities."

"Tell me, Holmes," I said, "what did Oswald believe in, in terms of politics?"

"Impossible to say, Watson. I am going to New Orleans partly to seek some answer to that, but I may leave no wiser than on our arrival. Oswald may have been the ultimate casualty of conflicting ideologies: the man who had ceased to believe in anything, politically speaking. You recall the curious entries in his 'Historic Diary' which he opened in October 1959 when he defected to Russia. It records his growing disenchantment with life in Russia, and with the regime there. By February 1961, Oswald was writing to the American Embassy in Moscow asking to return to the United States. By July he had obtained permission, after being subjected to searching interviews at the Embassy. We may be quite certain that during February and July, exhaustive inquiries took place, especially when it was observed that Oswald married a Russian, Marina Prusakova, in April 1961. Yet he seems to have obtained readmission quite swiftly after an interview in July. Indeed, he was deemed not to have expatriated himself, and his passport was returned to him. He would be 'de-briefed' in an extremely thorough manner, of that we may be sure, on his return to the West. The State Department would take note that he had worked in a large plant at Minsk manufacturing electronic parts and radio receivers. Wherever he moved in the United States, Oswald was henceforth under surveillance, and this he knew from sundry interrogations when he returned."

"Do I surmise, Holmes, that you believe Oswald may have been recruited by American counterespionage services on his return?"

"That I do not know, Watson. But one thing is clear. He was a possible candidate, though only in some very lowly capacity, by reason of his personal history, his defection, his stated views, and his Russian wife. We could put the question in another way. If American counterespionage circles did not see possibilities inherent in the recruitment of Oswald, in however lowly a capacity, then who on earth *would* they consider recruiting?"

"But Oswald was still a security risk."

"My dear Watson, you should know from some of our other cases that intelligence organizations today know how to guard themselves against risks. They have a battery of tests, checks and doublechecks—including deliberate traps. But more to the point, they do not put their own activities at risk when they receive intelligence from agents or contacts in the field. The safety apparatus is much too sophisticated for that to occur, except on rare occasions when a first class intellect manages to penetrate their defenses in the higher echelons. Oswald may have had a sharp, indeed a cunning mind, but it was cluttered and untutored. He could not spell, and he could hardly write coherent English. If he was recruited, it would be at a *very* low level indeed; no more than an occasional contact, and he was expendable, even disposable under certain circumstances in the pitiless world of espionage."

"But was not Oswald much too unstable a character to trust with *any* commission?"

"His known character could become part of his cover, and since his contributions would be sealed off from other activities, no great risks would be present. And remember, Watson, that agents always serve apprenticeships. They are tried out on harmless activities, well removed from the scene of essential operations, so that their shortcomings or failures can be noted before they are placed anywhere near what are termed, in the trade, 'sensitive areas.' Oswald was of a type to feel complimented, even thrilled by what would appear a special trust placed in him. No one would inform him that he was very small beer indeed."

"You feel, then, that he was recruited?"

"I merely say that I would be surprised if he were not contacted. Bear in mind that on the bottom rungs of the intelligence ladder, it matters little what the political beliefs of your recruits or informants may be. If they accord, in whole or part, with your adversary's beliefs, so much the better: the cover is more convincing, and there is less to be manufactured. The manufacture of a convincing life story is the most difficult part of placing an agent in the field, since the organizations they are meant to penetrate make their own searching inquiries before admitting the acolyte. In Oswald's case, little had to be manufactured. One could even wonder about the original defection, which did not last long by ordinary standards. As you may have noted, Oswald learned Russian during his military service in Japan and in California, up to the first few months of 1959. He defected later that same year. That is a short period in which to divest oneself entirely of the country of one's birth."

Holmes stood up and looked at his timepiece.

"We must be on our way, Watson. The car will take us to the airport. The driver has instructions and he will be outside in half an hour. Time to finish our packing. We will be discussing Mr. A. J. Hidell again, be sure of that."

10

Dusk was falling over the broad reaches of the delta as we circled above New Orleans to land at the airport on the shores of Lake Pontchartrain. Holmes's contacts in Washington rose to the occasion once more, and I was not altogether surprised when a chauffeur stepped forward as our luggage came through the barrier. His gloved hand came up in a discreet salute. *Sotto voce,* he enquired, "Mr. Sherlock Holmes, sir?"

Holmes inclined his head, and the chauffeur relieved us of our bags. We followed him through the vestibule, and he led us to a long sedan. We glided out of the airport without a sound. Once more, a thick glass screen separated us from the forward part of the car.

"I marvel at the efficiency of your arrangements, Holmes," I declared from the enfolding softness of the capacious fauteuil.

"The credit is not mine, Watson. Our clients supplied a telephone number in Washington. I call that number 'collect,' in the American parlance, from whatever location I happen to be in, and a nameless person responds to my wishes with remarkable promptitude, as you see. I do not doubt that the hotel will be extremely gracious, in a discreet location, our quarters comfortable. The hotel will be forwarding the bill to Washington, as at Dallas. It is an agreeable way to travel. By the way, Watson, you will sign your name as Dr. MacLennan, from Edinburgh University Medical School. You are a Scottish physician visiting colleagues at the Veterans' Administration Hospital here. It is close to the main library, and four or five blocks from Lafayette Square, whither we will be taking a stroll. I am Dr. Ferguson, of Westminster Hospital. Our work is on carcinogens."

"Do you not feel that your investigations in this city carry elements of danger, Holmes, even at this date?"

"One cannot be certain, Watson. No doubt you are recalling the unpleasant business of the Silo Forgeries on the waterfront, across the Mississippi River from the French Quarter here."

I was indeed. The case was many years ago, shortly after my marriage. I had not accompanied Holmes on that occasion, and he had traveled by sea. The case had involved an international grain swindle of stupendous proportions, with the forgery of ships' manifests and loading bills by ingenious trickery at the Customs offices. Holmes solved the case through his extraordinary knowledge of skilled forgery techniques, and by observing the minute but separate characteristics of two printing presses in different sections of this sprawling southern city. However, the ship bearing Holmes on his return journey after his solution of the case suffered an inexplicable explosion in its boiler room as it headed into the Gulf of Mexico. Had it not been for prompt manning of the lifeboats, Holmes would have been lost at sea, along with the other passengers on board. I could understand Holmes's caution on this occasion. The underworld, he had good reason to know, has a long memory and a long arm.

We were moving slowly down a narrow tree-lined street.

"This is the Old Quarter, Watson, the Vieux Carré: you must pronounce it Vo Carray if you stroll here and mix with the local residents. It is a colorful spot, with fine examples of French architecture in the colonial style. Observe the ironwork on the balconies above you. A most picturesque place."

The sedan drew into a quiet side street, where high walls of white stucco shielded tall, elegant houses with black shutters. I was reminded of Paris, and the streets behind the Boulevard Raspail, where the Grandes Ecoles and the better-placed ministries are juxtaposed to the choicer mansions of the ancien régime. The car stopped at a large wrought iron gate backed by black timber, the bollards suggesting a porte cochère. Our chauffeur tugged at a handle and a soft tinkling sounded somewhere within. The gates swung open without a sound. The car moved in, and the gates closed behind us. We stopped before two tall, heavy doors, their polished black surfaces catching the gleam of the coach lamps above.

The chauffeur pushed at one of the massive doors, and we entered. A moustachioed maître d'hôtel approached us. He was dressed in a short black morning coat and striped trousers, with a cravat at his neck. It was difficult to perceive that this was a hotel.

"Dr. Ferguson, Dr. MacLennan, good evening sirs," our host greeted us. The accent was indubitably of French extraction. We subscribed these names at a polished mahogany table to one side of a deep open hearth, where logs burned in a dog grate. Our host led us up a single flight of stairs, deeply carpeted in a warm plum-colored velour. The brass stair rods caught the light of the crystal chandelier in the stairwell.

We were quartered on the second floor, the shutters drawn across the french windows in an oval room furnished in Louis Quinze. When the porter had withdrawn, Holmes took a street map from the escritoire and spread it on the circular table beneath the central chandelier.

"We are located here, Watson. Tomorrow morning we will walk across Canal Street to Gravier Street. Here is Lafayette Square, where we will tarry. Observe the Post Office and, nearby, the Civic Center and public library. I must ask you to amuse yourself in those areas for perhaps an hour or more, at mid-morning. I am having discussions with one or two officials who are in a position to know more than most people about some curious political activities in and around Lafayette Square in the 1960s. But they have asked me to come alone. You do not mind, Watson?"

"Of course not, Holmes."

"You will be near your colleagues at the Veterans' Hospital if you care to walk a block for a busman's holiday," Holmes chuckled.

"Perhaps I will glance over it."

"Excellent. We can rendezvous later at the public library, where I have an engagement with the chief librarian."

We dined downstairs in a circular booth, the deep velvet drapes about us muffling our conversation. The immaculate waiters had stationed themselves discreetly by the chafing dishes at the end of the salon. We dined superbly, and then repaired to our suite, where the cognac was set out, a small silver spirit lamp warming the globes on either side. I took out my pipe and filled a bowl as we settled ourselves by an open fire. Holmes tossed a map at me, a detailed street map of New Orleans, and he indicated the streets and areas we would visit next day. He drew on his extraordinary memory to trace the names and landmarks we would pass. That done, we conversed for perhaps an hour or more, while Holmes puffed at his meerschaum, then retired early. We would have a busy day tomorrow, my companion averred.

Holmes took his morning bath soon after seven, and was already jotting down some *aides memoires* when I joined him. We had a simple breakfast of excellent coffee and croissants in our suite. Holmes handed me the map again to give me my bearings. We would stroll along Decatur Street near the French Market, then cross Canal to Magazine Street. Holmes wished to call in at the Post Office, where he had a brief errand, he said.

It was a fine, clear morning, and ships were unloading at the wharves beyond Decatur as we strolled. Out in the great brown waters of the Mississippi River, flat barges butted against the stream, their heavy cargoes bringing them almost level with the water. Above and about us, magnolia trees were shedding their leaves, but some gave occasional shade from the bright morning sunshine. Office workers on their way to work thronged the streets near the Custom House. We stopped outside a large building along Magazine Street. Legends above the doors showed it to be the main post office.

"I have a short appointment with the Postmaster," Holmes declared, "and I fear two English visitors may seem a trifle suspicious. You do not mind strolling a little further, Watson? Try a turn around Lafayette Square. The historical connections, old and new, are intriguing, be assured. I will find you somewhere about the square, on a bench, perhaps."

It was a balmy morning. After I had taken one or two turns around the square, I sat down, imbibing the warmth. Holmes joined me, and since he did not volunteer any remark on his errand as we walked on, I did not inquire. Our surroundings were mean and decrepit. The area had clearly seen better days: cheap bars and coffee houses, premises closed and partly vandalized. The untended, dusty wrecks of partly cannibalized cars adorned the side streets.

"Not quite what you expected to glorify a noble French soldier and statesman, Watson."

"Not at all, Holmes. I had expected something like Beacon Hill in Boston, to be frank, but this is redolent of lower Manhattan."

"And thus a good locale for the comings and goings of mercenaries and brigands, Watson. You cannot have villainous-looking men in boots and fatigues tramping through the more respectable sections of the city. Here, the locals took little notice of them—they are transients themselves. Ah, there it is."

We had stopped before a battered three-story building. A faded sign said that the Stevedores' and Longshoremen's Union had once been located here. Holmes checked the number on the door, 544 Camp Street. The side entrance to the same building was on Lafayette Street, number 531.

"Two distinct addresses, and one building, you observe, Watson."

"What follows, Holmes?"

"It was from one of these addresses, 544 Camp Street, that Oswald claimed to be organizing his pro-Castro Fair Play for Cuba Committee. When he distributed handbills in New Orleans in 1963 they bore this address. He had himself photographed and took part in a television discussion on his activities during 1963. The other entrance to the same building, 531 Lafayette Street, was the address of one Guy Banister, who ran a private detective business from this unprosperous spot in 1963. Mr. Banister was once employed by the FBI in their Chicago offices. He did not spend much time at his detective agency, but concentrated most of his efforts on behalf of an organization named the Anti-Communist League of the Caribbean. In fact Banister's office, and this building, were important ports of call for anti-Castro activities organized in three main cities during 1963—Miami, New Orleans, and Dallas, Texas. Elsewhere in New Orleans, Oswald was involved with anti-Castro activities."

"This is very curious," I observed. "Is your information reliable, Holmes?"

"It is. I have applied some checks already. I have an appointment this morning with a further source of information. By noon the picture will be fuller."

We walked around the west side of the square, and Holmes indicated another building to our left.

"That remains a Federal Building, Watson," he said enigmatically. "The other is no longer used for counter-espionage activity. It is to be demolished soon."

Some blocks away, the large, handsome public library was a pleasure to the eye. Acres of glass were married skillfully to fine stonework, the whole edifice gleaming in appearance, and a monument to civic pride. Inside, I found a pleasant nook giving on to a small interior water garden where tall fronds combined to create the illusion of a miniature landscape. Holmes left me here, and I browsed among travel books from the nearby shelves. He was gone for forty minutes, and when he returned I caught the familiar glint of interest in his eyes. We waited until we had left the building.

"Most intriguing," said Holmes. "I checked Oswald's borrowings from the library during 1963. Happily, the librarian had already undertaken the considerable task of retrieving all of Oswald's book borrowing, following the detailed investigation of his activities by the FBI immediately after the assassination. Oswald's tastes may interest you, Watson: very little that bears on his professed political faith; a little on philosophy, futuristic novels by Aldous Huxley; some historical works. But much more on spy stories and the world of espionage, including the world of one of my younger, fictional co-workers, Mr. James Bond. A courageous young buck, though somewhat of a hostage to the temptations of the flesh. Most unprofessional . . ."

I was not versed in the exploits of this character and so refrained from comment. I returned to an earlier theme of our discussions.

"Do I not recall, Holmes, that Oswald made a strenuous attempt to return to the Soviet Union in 1963, and that when this was denied to him, he sought to go to Cuba? Did he not actually make a visit to Mexico City in 1963, and did he not have an argument at the Consulate there about his wish to go to Cuba?"

"Indeed, Watson. But that does not necessarily point to a second defection. If we read Oswald's comments on the Soviet Union in his 'Historic Diary' and on the United States on his journey back, we must be very surprised indeed that he would ever wish to set foot in the Soviet Union again. Unless it was with a very special commission that appealed to his unusual makeup."

"I think I catch your drift, Holmes. Are you saying that his pro-Castro activities in New Orleans were a necessary part of building up a 'cover' for placing him in alien territory?"

"I am saying that his activities were not inconsistent with that. It was officially confirmed—as the Warren Commission's Report states—that Oswald's claim to have founded a chapter of the Fair Play for Cuba Committee was entirely false. Oswald's letters to the Communist Party of the United States contained equally spurious claims. So much is fact, and confirmed by the official records.

"Then on September 26, 1963, Oswald travelled by bus to Mexico City in order, it is said, to obtain entry visas to Cuba and to the Soviet Union. But the plot thickens, Watson, for there is on-the-spot evidence that it was not Oswald, but another man, impersonating Oswald, who visited the consular authorities. He was greatly agitated when the visas were refused. What plans were afoot? An attempt to put a spurious "Oswald" in touch with American agents in Cuba and in the Soviet Union? Or some darker, domestic design, with Oswald an unwitting dupe? Why did this "Oswald" seek to visit Moscow by way of Cuba? It remains a puzzle, unless "Oswald," or his mentors, sought to have the additional benefit of favorable reports from the Cuban authorities to the Russians on his activities in New Orleans. After all, Oswald would hardly be a welcome guest in Russia after his rejection of that country in favor of a return to the West. What could explain such a turnabout?"

A thought occurred to me.

"Holmes," I exclaimed, "Oswald must have received payments for any government services. If we could obtain details of Oswald's bank statements or tax returns for 1963, would they not shed light? He would hardly have carried out all this activity—whatever its purpose—without payments of some kind."

"Correct, Watson, although small payments could well have been in cash. Those were the first documents I wished to see on my visit to Washington, and unfortunately they are embargoed. I was not allowed to see them." Holmes was tight-lipped. He lapsed into silence. We had reached an intersection where traffic was plying up and down a long avenue.

"Here I must leave you for my second appointment, Watson, and then I may pay one or two brief further calls. I suggest you stroll back to the hotel, and I will join you for lunch. I also suggest you talk to no one at all—least of all any stranger who may attach himself to you, ostensibly to guide your steps to some tourist attraction. I was warned discreetly on the telephone this morning that our hotel at Dallas received a set of inquiries as to our presence, the calls from some unstated source. I left word at Dallas that we were returning directly to Washington. But it will pay us to be careful. That is why I have not told you my next rendezvous. I was requested not to do so, and if I should be delayed beyond 1:30, kindly inspect the yellow pages of the telephone directory in the writing desk in our room. In the section listing Television Rentals, under the letter H, you will find a number inscribed in pencil in a display advertisement. Telephone that number if I should be delayed unduly. It connects with Washington, D.C. Otherwise expect me at 12:30."

"Holmes," I expostulated, "are you sure you are not running into danger?"

"Certainly not at my rendezvous, I assure you Watson. The credentials of my contacts are impeccable. I take the precaution merely because of our stroll around the environs of Lafayette Square, and my visit to the Post Office. Walls sometimes have ears, and buildings always have eyes. I will see you for lunch, have no fear." With that, he hailed a cab and was gone.

I walked back by way of Chartres Street, pausing only briefly to admire the houses about Jackson Square. Happily the only solicitation I received was from an elderly man dressed as a minstrel, rattling his wooden collection box on behalf of some dusky musicians who strolled along the edge of the road playing brass instruments, with a heavy rhythmical beat on a drum, which was inscribed "Bourbon Street Ramblers." I placed some silver coins in the box, which the old gent rattled with a genial smile. Then I went on my way.

Holmes returned only slightly late. He arrived in our room soon after one o'clock. I sprang up and helped him off with his coat. He rubbed his hands together, as for a deed well accomplished, but it was soon clear that he intended to be taciturn. I did not inquire too closely. I knew that if Holmes carried confidences, his lips were sealed. But my curiosity could not be altogether contained.

"I do not ask you the identity of your discussant today, Holmes, but is he of the opinion that there was a conspiracy to kill the President?"

"Yes. At a very high level, in his opinion. But I do not share that view—not so far, at any rate, and at times I felt he pushed his case to extremes. He holds, for instance, that on the day of the assassination sinister forces in Washington rushed the President's body from Texas so that the State authorities could not conduct a post mortem on the bullet wounds. But in fact it was the President's aides and his family who ordered out the body over the protests of the local authorities. I am not ready to believe that the murder was the work of an 'alternative government' seizing power in Washington. In such a case, it would have had to work hand in glove with the local police, local agents of the FBI and also the Secret Service. Exceedingly improbable. Nevertheless, the man I talked with today is a responsible and concerned citizen with a sound legal training, and much experience of the law. He was a colleague and confidant of a New Orleans District Attorney whose views were entirely ignored by the Warren Commission, even though he knew more of Oswald's life and movements here in New Orleans than anyone in the public eye."

"I am intrigued, Holmes," I interjected, seeking to draw him out. But Holmes switched the topic of conversation.

"Oswald claimed to numerous individuals here in New Orleans—to the police, to television reporters, to various members of the Cuban community—that he had formed a local chapter of the Fair Play for Cuba Committee, a perfectly legal, national association, with a head office in New York; and that he had some thirty to forty members in his chapter. There was no such local chapter. Oswald's claim was false. All the resources of the police, the local agents and special agents of the FBI, as well as the Secret Service, quite apart from independent investigators, failed to unearth any such chapter. Oswald was unable to give any evidence of its existence, even though he was proclaiming its existence quite publicly to the press and even on a radio interview, in the summer of 1963. Then there was the curious location of his office at 544 Camp Street, proclaimed on the handbills he distributed. In fact he used an office there, but I have ascertained from two independent sources that the same building housed a well-organized anti-Castro group, supported by Cuban émigrés driven from Cuba by Mr. Castro's régime."

"Was any of this information known to members of the Warren Commission?"

"In part, yes. Testimony is contained in their own volumes of evidence—at the end of Volume 22, if my memory serves. A number of depositions are given there from individuals in New Orleans, including the gentleman who leased the offices in the building at Camp Street. There is also testimony from an important witness in Volume 10—one has to locate the different strands of evidence in different volumes to piece the pattern together.

"This witness, a Mr. Carlos Bringuier, was a lawyer in Cuba until he fled the country in 1961, and became a leading member of the anti-Castro organization in this city. He testified that one day in August 1963 Oswald approached him with an offer to help in the fight against Castro. He offered to train guerrillas for the fight, even offered to fight himself, and loaned to Mr Bringuier his Marine Corps manual on tactics. But four days later, Oswald was to be found in another part of New Orleans, in Canal Street, with a placard around his neck, distributing handbills urging Fair Play for Cuba and inviting members of the public to join his fictitious local chapter. He was unlikely to recruit any outside the International Trade Market—the very heart of New Orleans business enterprise. But he was certain to attract attention at that location, and indeed he did. His photograph appeared in the local press as an agitator for the Castro government. It was this scene, photographed by television and newspaper cameramen, that led to an altercation between Mr. Bringuier, two of his associates, and Oswald. The brawl was sufficient to bring about arrests and appearances in court. It seems clear that Oswald urged Bringuier to hit him and that Oswald wanted above all to secure publicity for his pro-Castro activities."

"Did he succeed?"

"He did indeed. About ten days after his fine in court for disturbing the peace, he was invited to expound his beliefs on a radio program in New Orleans. He debated these with the other guest on the program, the Director of a curiously named organization, 'The Information Council of the Americas,' a virulently anti-Communist and anti-Castro group in the city. I was occupied with some documentary evidence on these matters this morning. Suffice to say that by the end of August 1963, Oswald had obtained newspaper and radio publicity in New Orleans as a self-declared Marxist and the chief organizer of a pro-Castro committee here. There is one difficulty attending the public persona Oswald had thus established, however."

"And what is that?"

"A confidential informant of the FBI in New Orleans who kept close watch on the pro-Castro organizations in the city reported that Oswald was unknown to him. Another regular informant specializing in the local activities of the Communist Party also testified that Oswald was unknown. Another informant again, a self-declared delegate of the Cuban Revolutionary Council in New Orleans, stated that Oswald was unknown to him. So Oswald's pro-Castro activities were singular, in a very literal sense.''

"Most strange, Holmes."

"Even stranger, my dear Watson. If we cast about in the other volumes among the Commission's exhibits, in Volume 20 we find Oswald writing during that same month of August to the officers of *The Worker,* in New York City, drawing attention to his activities in New Orleans, referring to the publicity he had received in the press and on the radio, and offering his services as a photographer—a trade in which he could claim some skill and experience. He mentioned in his letter that he intended to relocate himself in the New York area. He also wrote to the Communist Party in New York on September 1, 1963, asking how he might contact the Party in the Baltimore-Washington area, as he planned to move there shortly."

"Might this not merely indicate that he was indeed a dedicated Marxist, seeking to become a comrade in the Communist groups organized in the New York area?"

"It is not so simple as that, Watson. Among those Oswald was in touch with in New Orleans was a Mr. David Ferrie. Does that name mean anything to you?"

"It does not."

"I felt sure it would not. It is most curious that he was not called to testify to the Warren Commission. He was a highly intelligent defrocked priest who spoke several languages and was a skilled pilot. He lived in this city, but was constantly leaving in his private plane at short notice for mysterious destinations in the Caribbean."

"What was his trade?"

"Gun running. Delivering arms from anti-Castro groups in New Orleans and other spots in Louisiana and Texas."

"But what was the connection with Oswald?"

"A diligent search of the Commission's volumes of evidence (the Index mentions him erroneously as an item in Volume 7, whereas it is located in Volume 8: a printer's error no doubt) confirms that the investigating authorities in New Orleans had established a connection between Oswald and this mercenary, a connection going back to Oswald's school days in New Orleans in the 1950s, when Oswald joined the Civil Air Patrol as a cadet. The man in charge of that Patrol was this brigand Mr. Ferrie. In the 1960s he was very active in the New Orleans area, a flamboyant character much in the news, but only locally, not nationally. Tracing his movements clearly gave the police and local agents of the FBI a good deal of trouble. Ferrie often boasted to those about him that he was employed by the Central Intelligence Agency."

"Why did not the Commission call him as a witness?"

"Why not, indeed? I know not. But that is now idle speculation."

"How so?"

"He was found dead in February 1967, with two suicide notes in his room, although my informant of today observes that the signatures on the suicide notes were typed, not written in his own hand—a very curious last rite for a literate man. If, indeed, Ferrie typed them."

"Have you been able to establish any connection between Oswald and the CIA?"

"The trail is very cold now."

I attempted a more hopeful tack.

"There were other suggestions, were there not, Holmes, that Oswald was an informant for the FBI?"

Holmes stirred. "There were indeed. That is one of the leads I wished to follow up here."

"Any success?"

"A pervasive silence. It is most unsatisfactory."

My own memory was jogged suddenly, and I brought up something I recalled from my reading of the bulky tome Holmes had pressed into my hands for overnight reading in Dallas.

"Did not Mr. J. Edgar Hoover, the Director of the FBI, sign an affidavit that Oswald was never employed, or paid, or recruited by the FBI in any capacity whatever? I have a distinct memory of that."

"Your memory serves you correctly, Watson. The affidavit, and other declarations by Mr. Hoover, are set out fully in the volumes of evidence. He came forth with it at an early date in the deliberations of the Commission, on February 6, 1964, in fact, and a very persuasive statement it was. A week later Mr. Hoover wrote again to the Commission, this time enclosing with his letter ten affidavits signed by all the local agents of the FBI at Dallas and New Orleans who would have been responsible for, or would have knowledge of, any attempt to develop Oswald as an FBI informant. Note Mr. Hoover's remarks, Watson. *All* agents who would have knowledge of any attempt to develop Oswald as an FBI informant."

"But the affidavits must surely put the matter to rest, Holmes? We are surely not at liberty to doubt the sworn statements of federal agents?"

"We are not. But there were curious lacunae among the ten affidavits Mr. Hoover so helpfully provided to the Commission. We must first apply our minds to the exact wording of the affidavits. What our French colleagues term *'scrutin de texte.'* Mr. Hoover and his agents in the field insisted that they did not attempt to *develop* Oswald as an informant. The word 'develop' is common parlance in the Bureau. It means a systematic process, through time. The agents might well claim that they had not attempted to 'develop' Oswald as an informant. That does not mean that they were not in contact with him from time to time, seeking information. Certainly he was interviewed by FBI agents on sundry occasions. The agents admit this."

"So the affidavits may be circumspect?"

"A trifle, possibly. But there is a more important matter. Several agents who were closely connected with Oswald's activities in New Orleans and in Dallas did not submit affidavits. Mr. Hoover did not allude to them."

"Good heavens!" I exclaimed. "Who were they?"

"In Dallas, Special Agent Vincent Drain had responsibilities for checking on individuals in the area who were security risks. It was his task to investigate those who might threaten violence during the period of the President's visit. Mr. Drain was busy as early as October in checking on possible sources of threats to the President. The Dallas and nearby Fort Worth offices of the FBI had a considerable amount of information on Lee Oswald as a known defector—indeed, agents of the FBI had interviewed Oswald in 1962 and on subsequent dates. So much so that by November 1963, Oswald was clearly somewhat harassed by local FBI agents. Mr. Drain was an important special agent. On the day of the assassination he delivered the alleged murder weapon to the Dallas police department for inspection, as well as spent cartridge cases from the Texas School Book Depository. Thereafter he took affidavits from the senior members of the Police Department. Perhaps Mr. Drain was too busy or too important a man to be interviewed by the Commission among their 550 witnesses. A pity. He probably knew more about the vital details surrounding the case than any official in the vicinity. Another local agent, Mr. Bardwell Odum, was equally parsimonious in his help to the Commission. He did not testify."

"And the other agents you mention?"

"A Mr. Milton Kaack and a certain Mr. Warren De Brueys, who appear behind the testimony of several witnesses in New Orleans and in Dallas. As early as 1962, and right through the summer of 1963, their primary duties were clearly to trace, perhaps to infiltrate, the extremist organizations in this city. Several witnesses testified to the Commission that De Brueys was often seeking information from them: Mr. Carlos Bringuier, the émigré lawyer, asserted that Mr. Warren De Brueys was familiar to many of the Cuban émigrés in New Orleans —a testimony confirmed by the witnesses Mr. Orest Pena and Mr. Ruperto Pena, his brother. We passed the location of the Habana Bar owned by these gentlemen in 1963 as we made our way along Decatur Street today, beyond the waterfront. We may believe these various witnesses when they testify to frequent visits by Mr. De Brueys. The Pena brothers were clearly anxious to cooperate with the FBI and served as informants. As you may imagine, owners of bars often make valuable informants, because of the number of people they see come and go. There is what is called a 'trade-off' for the owners of bars —the authorities can choose to treat them lightly, even look the other way, in the matter of minor disturbances on the premises if customers become obstreperous or the worse for drink. Bar owners and bartenders also provide bridges to the fringes of the underworld where the police and the FBI gain their 'tip-offs.' "

"I begin to see the ramifications," I observed.

"Nevertheless, the Pena brothers, and Bringuier, clearly felt somewhat harassed by the FBI agent Mr. De Brueys. They wished to be left alone to get on with their business. Another witness, Mr. Dean Andrews, a lawyer in New Orleans, also confirmed that Mr. De Brueys was much involved with keeping traces on extremist political activities in the city. Oswald's activities were known to the agent, without a shadow of a doubt. It was a pity that Mr. Andrews' testimony was not followed up, considering some vital leads he provided. He clearly knew a great deal about the more exotic aspects of New Orleans social and cultural life, and something of the private lives of those who mixed with Oswald. Mr. Andrews was also an expert with firearms, after five years as an ordnanceman in the United States Navy during military service."

"Did he reveal something important?"

"His testimony gives the clear impression that he was convinced Oswald could not have shot the President. He refers to three people who did not come before the Commission: a Mexican, another individual by the name of Clay Bertrand, and the person who shot the President."

"The assassin?" I said incredulously.

"In Mr. Andrews' belief, yes, although Andrews was

not an impressive witness, despite being a member of the Louisiana Bar. An exotic character."

"Did the Commission locate these men?"

"It seems they were not interested, and the local FBI agent insisted to Mr. Andrews that he had never met a person named Mr. Bertrand; that he was a figment of the lawyer's imagination. Yet the details of meetings with Mr. Bertrand are very specific and graphic as to time, place, and circumstance. It is difficult to imagine why Mr. Andrews should have made up this character."

"Why then did the Commission not seek to trace him?"

"The FBI agents stated that they did so, but that no trace of any such person emerged."

"Did the agent Mr. De Brueys testify to that?"

"Alas, there was no testimony, not even an affidavit from Mr. De Brueys."

"Did other agents in the area submit affidavits?"

"Indeed yes. In New Orleans and at Dallas. The period Oswald lived in New Orleans—spring and summer of 1963—is clearly crucial. Mr. Hoover wrote that all agents having any connection with or knowledge about Oswald had rendered affidavits. That could not have been an accurate statement."

"But you have not encountered any direct evidence indicating that Oswald met this agent De Brueys?"

"There is a cryptic entry in the address book found among Oswald's possessions that baffled the investigators and cryptographers who studied the entry, which is clearly in Oswald's hand. It is written in Russian characters, but they are poorly formed. The entry reads either 'Debroy' or 'Deboovy.' Oswald was extremely weak at spelling, even phonetically. There may be a connection with Mr. De Brueys. It is difficult to place any other name to such a curious entry, and the address book relates closely to Oswald's New Orleans phase."

"Does this agent appear anywhere in the evidence presented to the Commission?"

"In a disconnected fashion, yes. He makes a discreet entry only three weeks after the assassination, when he interviewed the mayor of Dallas, Mr. Cabell, about his administrative actions following the shooting of Oswald by Mr. Jack Ruby."

"The mayor was not under suspicion?"

"Not at all. Mr. Cabell was named as an enemy of the people in a vitriolic handbill circulated by extreme right-wing forces in the city on the eve of the President's visit. His name and his views were coupled with the policies of the President.

"But come, Watson. Dallas is behind us, and now our work is finished in this city also. At other times I would have liked to show you more of it. It is exceedingly beautiful in parts. And I would that we might have taken a ride together on the *Delta Queen.*"

"The *Delta Queen?*" I was puzzled by my companion's reference.

"A boat of surpassing beauty, Watson, which plies on this great river here. A regal lady, with teak handrails and mahogany paneling, stained glass windows and much British oak in her bowels. She was built on the Clyde. But now, Watson, we must prepare to leave for New York this afternoon."

"New York!" I gasped. "My dear Holmes, you forget that there is a threat to your life if you should set foot in that city."

"That is why we will take an evening flight, landing

after dark. We should be in our hotel shortly before midnight. I arranged matters by a call to Washington from a public telephone box on my way here. Come, we will first enjoy a delicious lunch here, and the car will collect us at mid-afternoon. All is arranged."

"Might I ask the reason for this change of plans, Holmes?" I inquired.

"Time enough to tell you when we are airborne, Watson. Recall my earlier admonitions on the need for minimum information, in case some unpleasantness befalls either of us. I observed a gentleman in dark glasses taking an unusual interest in my work at the library, and then at the Records building as I checked Oswald's reading matter in the summer of 1963. I shook him off by dint of two changes of direction in a taxi cab. But it is time we departed. The French Quarter is very cosmopolitan, but strangers on the streets do not go unseen."

Holmes must have caught my look of alarm.

"Cheer up, Watson. Our maitre d'hôtel is not quite what he seems. He is trustworthy. He spent twenty years with the French Bureau de Sécurité. He knows our mission, and we are well guarded. Let us enjoy our lunch."

11

Holmes elected to remain silent on the reason for our visit to New York, and I did not tax him on the subject. He was clearly wrapped in thought, and I knew better than to disturb his cogitation. Our flight was smooth and uneventful. At New York, a limousine awaited us. Despite a taciturn greeting on the part of the chauffeur, I thought that I detected a Scotch accent as the driver took our hand luggage. Holmes responded to the greeting as the driver held open the rear door.

"You must find this city somewhat strange after Edinburgh," he remarked.

The chauffeur started visibly.

"How did you know I was from Edinburgh, sir?"

"Is not your lapel button the insignia of a famous Scottish football team—Hibernians?"

The man looked down at the diminutive button in his lapel. I had barely noticed its presence.

"Och, I thought you must have sixth sense, sir. Yes indeed, that brings back the old country to me."

"And does the Minister keep you busy at the United Nations?"

"Fairly busy, sir. It varies." He closed the door.

"This is the British Minister's car, Holmes?" I queried.

"They told you at Washington, no doubt."

"No, my dear Watson. They did not specify. That would be unnecessary—and unwise, given our destination today. An elementary matter. The limousine is of British manufacture: very necessary in this very competitive city, where import and export markets engage in a war of attrition. At the United Nations, our resident Minister could hardly afford to go about his diplomatic business in a car of American or any other foreign make. The Scottish driver completes the picture—together with the small United Nations parking permit on the windscreen."

"I had not observed, Holmes."

"The insignia are discreet, but they are there. I gathered from my telephone call to Washington that the Foreign Office would take over our dispositions in this dangerous city. A change of plans is always useful to break a pattern."

Our limousine sped smoothly in the middle lane of broad concrete highways sweeping us toward the brightly lit, crenellated skyline of Manhattan that now lay before us. We crossed a bridge and entered the heart of the city, the car dipping fore and aft as we encountered small chasms in the tarmacadam. Yellow taxi cabs surged on either side of us as we traveled down and then across town for a few blocks. I recognized Fifth Avenue and beyond, in the night, the broad stygian mass of Central Park. The car stopped outside an elegant hotel giving on to the southern end of the Park.

The driver took our bags into the lobby, then, with a salute, disappeared as quietly and efficiently as he had arrived. Holmes had already informed me that on this occasion I would retain my own name. He had refrained from telling me his own chosen incognito, but as he signed the register I noted with wry amusement that he had chosen the name Professor Moriarty. I held my tongue until we were safely inside our suite on the top floor, overlooking the Park. When the door was closed, I could not restrain an exclamation.

"You have chosen a bizarre alias, if I may say so, Holmes."

Holmes chuckled, a trace of devilment in his tone. "Perhaps a touch of sentiment, my dear Watson, since this is certainly my last case. I clashed with Moriarty on sundry occasions, as you know, and more than once the villain came near to worsting me. At the end, there was a degree of mutual respect."

"Is it possible to learn now what brings us to this city, Holmes?" My apprehensions were not allayed by the slight air of levity my companion had introduced into the proceedings. Perhaps it was the swift pace of the metropolis that had brought on this access of humor.

However, Holmes became serious once more, and lowered his voice to a sepulchral level.

"I wish to examine the originals of some letters Oswald wrote to organizations in this city. I have seen photocopies deposited in the National Archives, and some indeed are printed in the published volumes of evidence and exhibits. But photocopies are not the same as the originals. They show the line, but not the actual character of the writing on the page. Nor does it show the quality of the paper. As you know from many of our cases, Watson, a piece of writing paper is a mine of information: it is an artifact with a history of its own, telling a good deal about the sender's tastes, habits, the state of his pocket. Sometimes, indeed, the smell of the surroundings become absorbed into the paper itself—you will recall the unmistakable odor on the threatening letters written from a dispensary, in the case of the missing hallucinogens in Bristol? In this case, alas, no such clues can be expected: the scent will be very cold. Nevertheless, other characteristics should be preserved on the page."

"The matter is not one of possible forgery?"

"No. I am satisfied on that point. I have compared Oswald's writing on numerous examples where the authenticity is not in doubt. But a person's handwriting changes from day to day—almost from hour to hour, according to mood, the pressures of time and place, the daily round. You will have observed, Watson, when your bank returns your checks, that a dozen signed checks reflect a dozen different moods in the writing on the check and even in the appended signature. With a letter, especially a letter composed at a time of stress on a difficult or contentious subject, the clues are all the more manifest."

"Will I accompany you on your search, Holmes?" I inquired eagerly.

Holmes held up a restraining hand.

"Alas, Watson. To my regret once more, that is not possible. The holders of the letters insist that I alone may view them. They do so reluctantly, as they demanded to know my identity, and this was disclosed to them."

"But Holmes," I expostulated, "does this not increase the danger of your presence in this city, where you are under a threat to your life?"

"Fear not, Watson. The very last thing sought by the persons I shall be seeing tomorrow is publicity of any kind. They belong to political organizations and publications that prefer to keep a very low profile, to borrow the parlance here, so that prudence dictates discretion. But apart from that, they are the very last persons in this teeming city to be consorting with the criminal element, since that is the canker they wish to root out of the capitalist system. No, Watson, I am looking forward to my meetings tomorrow, and I only regret that you cannot accompany me. Nevertheless, you could do me a valuable service if you would kindly undertake some research at the excellent New York Public Library."

"By all means, Holmes. What do you require?"

"I would be grateful if you would bring yourself up to date on some aspects of forensic medicine so that we can discuss a contentious matter. In particular, I would like to discuss the several effects of a bullet hitting the human skull. Whether there is an instant shattering effect, because of the disposition of the cranial plates, especially in what is termed the occipito-parietal region, or whether there is a tendency for a missile to enter with a clean hole at the point of entry, with the main damage to the skull at the point of exit."

"Most certainly, Holmes. Indeed I think I can do better. I have an American acquaintance in this city who is a good friend from medical school more years ago than I care to remember. We still exchange Christmas cards. He went on to Harvard Medical School, and he had a distinguished career at the Mayo Clinic before taking an emeritus position at the Bellevue Hospital here. I will ask his advice tomorrow morning. He will direct my steps to the best sources."

"Capital, Watson. We will start early tomorrow. We leave for Washington on the following day. We must conserve our energy meantime, so I bid you goodnight."

Holmes vanished to his room. I sat for a while, enjoying a pipe. The noises of the city reached into our sitting room, penetrating the thick double windows. Our sleep would be punctuated with the obbligatos of police car sirens throughout the night, the sharp ullulations rending the air in a city where night and day merged in sleepless consort.

I awoke to find a note from Holmes on the table in our sitting room. It proposed that we meet for tea at the Plaza Hotel at four o'clock. He was already about his business, so I ordered breakfast and digested the *New York Times*. Room service responded swiftly and efficiently, and I soon demolished the bacon and eggs on the chafing dishes. I looked up the address of my medical acquaintance of yesteryear, and as the time was shortly after nine o'clock, I first tried his town house. A servant informed me that the physician left for his office at the Bellevue Hospital at eight. This did not altogether surprise me, knowing his energies, and it took only another two or three minutes to locate him. At once I found myself almost caught up in that overwhelming warmth and generosity which are so much the mark of the people in this Republic. Although he was now a widower, it was all I could do to prevent a series of invitations to his home to meet friends and colleagues. With what firmness I could muster, I explained that my time was regrettably short, but gladly accepted his kind invitation to lunch. Within minutes, my old colleague had sketched the specialist collections available in the city to meet my request. Even before I descended to the hotel lobby to have a cab summoned, I knew that the best available literature to meet my query was already being called from the archives of one of the finest collections on forensic medicine in the world. This, thanks to the good offices of a friend whom I had last encountered at a congress almost a decade ago.

By mid-morning, I was immersed in the details, somewhat gruesome and vividly illustrated, of the latest research in the pathology of head wounds and missile entry to the cranial cavities. When I closed the books and monographs, it was a refreshing change to turn from my researches to the warm welcome of my host for lunch.

I will spare the reader the details of our conversations together, since these concerned old friends, and the pranks of medical school students many decades ago, when the world seemed a larger, and a safer place. Suffice to say that I was not at all surprised to find that at an advanced age, and true to the vigor of his fellow-countrymen, my companion could still enthuse about the delights of skiing in the mountains of New Hampshire, where he was born and raised, and where he planned to spend a holiday that following summer, canoeing with young men and women half a century younger than himself. My host showed traces of curiosity in my unusual request of that morning, but as he also knew of my association with Holmes—indeed, he had once been of inestimable assistance, by transatlantic telephone, he did not press his queries. I departed warmed and cheered by his hospitality.

Holmes was taking tea, ensconced in a corner of the lounge at the Plaza when I joined him. He poured me a cup after stirring the pot, and apologized for the strange contraption of a sachet of tea leaves suspended by a thread within the teapot—a device resembling a drowned mouse and designed, it seems, for trapping the tea leaves the better to jettison them and thus save labor. Holmes came straight to the point.

"What of your researches, Watson?"

"I have gathered a good deal of the latest findings, Holmes, and have made some sketches."

"Excellent. We will study them at the hotel later or, better still, when we have returned to Washington. I wish to compare them with some of the official exhibits."

"And what of your own discoveries, Holmes?"

Holmes looked about him swiftly.

"Perhaps we should not discuss matters further in this place. Walls often have ears, as you know, and I suspect that I was followed from the spot where I examined some interesting documents this morning. But the combination of Express and Local subway trains on a single platform is useful for evading the curious."

We thus fell to discussing trifles, until Holmes rose and summoned the page boy. We paid the bill and strolled to the lower end of Central Park where, opposite our hotel, a row of horsedrawn four-wheelers awaited custom.

"Our conversation will be safer in a barouche," observed Holmes.

We picked our way through the busy cross-stream of traffic, and Holmes engaged the first of the chariots. We were soon proceeding through the undulating twists and bends of the thoroughfare beneath the trees, our conversation low and contained, as traffic sped past us. Holmes took up my earlier question on his researches that day.

"Some small revelations, Watson. A letter is a mirror

of the subconscious, as you appreciate. The notions and suggestions that present themselves, the giveaway phrases, the order and the progression of ideas that come to the conscious mind—all these are testaments to the preoccupations beneath. As love letters provide clues to the yearnings, aspirations, and the fears of lovers, so the letters I scrutinized today, written by Oswald at a time of considerable mental stress and in a state of indecision, provide clues not merely to his beliefs, but to his state of mind."

"You intrigue me, Holmes. Can you furnish any examples?"

"Several." At this, I knew that he was about to draw on his capacious memory. He continued.

"In relating his fictitious activity for an alleged New Orleans chapter of the Fair Play for Cuba Committee, Oswald remarked on his supposed New Orleans office in a letter written to the New York Committee in the summer of 1963, 'Even if the office stays open for only 1 month, more people will find out about the F.P.C.C. than if there had never been any office at all. . . .' This is the sort of phrase that deserves the closest scrutiny, drawing on our knowledge of psychology, rather than graphology. A subconscious intention is present. I fastened on the phrase 'only 1 month.' The escapade is regarded as finite. So what is its purpose? To secure the necessary publicity before penetrating organizations at home or abroad? Possibly.

"As scholars and academicians know well, you cannot do better than examine the original documents, for reasons that emanate from the contents. My task this morning was to recreate the state of mind of Lee Oswald in the vital months of April to September 1963, a month before the assassin, or assassins, struck at Dallas on that grisly day."

The four-wheeler proceeded in its leisurely fashion, conducive to quiet conversation. I was ready to give Holmes the results of my own researches that day, but he held up his hand.

"It will be best, Watson, to reserve your observations until we have returned to Washington. I wish you to compare your own notes with the printed testimony of the physicians who attended the President as his life ebbed away in the Parkland Hospital at Dallas. There has been much disagreement—even conflicting expert testimony—on the crucial matter of whether all the shots struck the President from the rear, or whether one shot struck the President from the front, and I suggest that you study that testimony and the exhibits first before we discuss the matter further. If three shots came from the rear, perhaps they did not all emanate from the Texas School Book Depository. Bear this in mind. At present, my thoughts are upon Oswald's motives in choosing his alias 'A.J. Hidell' for his ostensible political activities in New Orleans, for the purchase of two weapons, and for the receipt of mail."

"Have you any hypothesis, Holmes?"

"A number of hypotheses. It is a commonplace that an individual can have many reasons for assuming an alias —and of course Oswald assumed at least two aliases when he resided at Dallas under the names Hidell and Lee for a period in 1963. There are no clear answers to the questions posed by these concurrent factors, Watson. The members of the Warren Commission offered no suggestions on this matter, and I confess I myself have no firm conclusions. But they existed, so indubitably an explanation for them also exists."

"It is not like you, Holmes, to be without a theory."

"No indeed, Watson. I can acquaint you with two or three at this instant. Assume Oswald needed an alias to shield himself from unwanted publicity for his political activities in certain quarters. However, this thesis encounters the difficulty that he positively sought publicity —as boldly and as provocatively as possible in the summer of 1963—using his own name of Lee Oswald. At the same time, the broadsheets he distributed in the streets bore the name 'A.J. Hidell' as the self-styled President of the fictitious local Chapter he claimed to advertise. So we must dismiss the most obvious original hypothesis—that Oswald wished to conceal his person and his identity in every way. Both the name of Oswald, and to a lesser extent the name Hidell, had been thoroughly broadcast on the news media in New Orleans by the end of August 1963, with a court appearance, photographs, press and radio coverage, all in his real name, and a fine on Oswald for disturbing the peace, for good measure.

"If the first hypothesis will not stand, we must proceed to an alternative one. Oswald wished, or perhaps he needed, to create a fictitious personality to cloak his own identity for some task or a set of tasks. What those were, or were intended to be, we can only conjecture. They could be of malevolent or incendiary intent; they could equally be designed for intended service to some organization or agency, so far as he was informed, whether he was misguided in this or not. The question is, which explanation fits the available facts? If we are in the world of espionage, we have a difficult task, since the central clues are not in our hands, nor are they likely to be furnished to us, for reasons of state. I confess that I have formed no firm judgment on this matter, but one thing we may reasonably conclude."

"And what is that?"

"If Oswald was being trained for espionage work, at however lowly a level, and if then, for some reason we do not know, he became the prime suspect in the murder of the President, the agencies who were in the process of recruiting him would place a very high premium on covering his tracks, and their own involvement, as quickly and as effectively as possible, in case public commentators drew any inferences on cause and effect between the initial recruitment and the final tragedy at Dallas."

"I see your point, Holmes. If Oswald shot the President, the very last thing any government agency would wish is that the killer should become known as their own agent."

"Exactly. And it is at that level, Watson, that reasons of state could be invoked, especially after the killer himself—real, or assumed—was done to death and was thus beyond testifying, so that no further questions could be put. As you know, Oswald's last forty-eight hours of interrogation yielded not a word of testimony. A most mystifying aspect of the case. The Dallas police, the Federal Bureau of Investigation, and the Secret Service have volunteered not a word on the testimony obtained during the several investigations undergone by Oswald. A most bizarre aspect of a case claiming the attention of the nation and the world—given that all of these agencies are meant to be the servants of the Republic."

"What other hypotheses have presented themselves?"

"One that we cannot discard is that Oswald came to see himself as a man of two worlds, the West and the East, owing fealty to neither, but becoming more and more tortuously involved in some romantic private notion that he could wreak revenge on both the systems which—on the basis of much that he wrote in his private diaries and in his letters—he had come to reject equally. It is possible that his actions on the 22nd of November 1963 were gestures of contempt and despair, an unheroic farewell by one who became a casualty of opposed political systems."

"This thesis begins to sound plausible, if I may say so, Holmes," I interjected.

"In saying so, Watson, I fear you risk emulating the members of the official Commission, whose Report we have been considering. These worthy gentlemen were clearly drawn to the simple, single hypothesis of the lone, demented assassin. It is appealing since it closes off all other avenues of inquiry. But it overlooks the behavior of the assassin before and after he became the prime suspect. His vehement protests of innocence, as I have already observed, sit oddly with the notion of the valedictory gesture of contempt and despair. If that thesis were to hold any truth, why not a ringing declaration by Oswald when he was presented to the world press on the night he was apprehended? No, Watson, I fear we must return to the murkier depths of our conjectures to date."

Ahead of us now I observed the busy traffic of the street at the lower end of the Park as our carriage brought us back to our point of departure. I paid the driver and waited with Holmes until the traffic lights allowed us to step briskly across lanes clogged with motorists departing their places of work. Looking about me, I wondered again at the curious and marvelous spectacle of this unique city with its soaring buildings, its hard-pressed citizens eking out a precarious existence in the game of getting and spending, and I allowed myself comforting thoughts of the solitude of our newly purchased stone-house, embowered in a combe in Dorset, to which I would soon retire in order to take up the gentle sport of angling.

"Come along, Watson." It was Holmes, jerking my arm as we threaded our way through traffic snarled between an interminable stream of buses and cars to the hotel beyond, where we were quartered.

That evening, we dined together at an excellent Hungarian restaurant on the upper east side of Manhattan, after two swift changes of taxi cab and a detour. Holmes agreed that he was taking a risk but, as we dined, I equally agreed with his observation, "This is the sort of food and wine, Watson, which one would cheerfully accept as the price for one's execution at dawn. Let us therefore enjoy it, whatever might befall us tonight."

A superb dinner, enlivened by gypsy music, put Holmes in a mood of reminiscence. He drew on his memory to summon back details of a case we had worked on together in Transylvania, where Holmes had his penultimate encounter with the fiendish Professor Moriarty, not long before the final, even more momentous encounter at the Reichenbach Falls, near Meiringen in Switzerland. Holmes had never confided to me whether or not he had plunged his arch-enemy down the abyss. It became clear, even as we dined and wined, the grape moving him to an unusual loquacity, that he chose to take this private secret to the grave, and I restrained my curiosity.

We returned by cab, and enjoyed a pipe and shared some excellent malt whiskey in our sitting room overlooking Central Park. Holmes brought his mind back to the case in hand and discoursed further on the problems it still presented, even to one with his acute powers of deduction.

"Our problem is twofold, Watson. We lack certain vital pieces of evidence, yet we are overwhelmed with a mountain of evidence—much of it pointing in quite different directions. We were speaking of Oswald's character and motives in the barouche in the Park this afternoon. One thesis I did not advance, because I have no knowledge to support it. You are aware that in the 1960s, the Central Intelligence Agency was experimenting with some very potent drugs, which were used on unsuspecting citizens. I am not opposed in principle to drugs. As you know, I occasionally allow myself an extremely weak solution of cocaine, rarely more than a seven per cent solution—but I have expert medical advice and know the chemistry. But during the 1960s, the Central Intelligence Agency was clearly operating in a void, with a whole series of drugs and serums whose effects had not been appraised scientifically. Some drugs were designed to induce the recipients to carry out deeds they would not remember afterwards.

"You have not had time, Watson, to extend your researches to an alarming aspect of the CIA's experimentation with drugs on unwitting members of the public. The "MK Ultra" program, in its operational side, sought ways to induce permanent amnesia for specific kinds of activity after particularly sensitive operations were completed. The program got out of hand, and the Inspector General of the CIA called for its abolition in his 1963 report."

"1963?" I queried.

"Yes. The program by then had had a ten-year life."

"Most alarming, Holmes. Are the experiments recorded in any archive?"

"I fear not. In 1973 the Director of the CIA ordered all the "MK Ultra" files to be destroyed. By chance a file was overlooked, and discovered by a resourceful writer named Mr. John Marks."

Not for the first time, I was staggered by Holmes's detailed knowledge of matters going well beyond the case in hand.

"But we must put these unpleasant aspects aside, Watson," he continued. "There is nothing we can deduce from them now. I mention them merely to indicate the stray leads that have accumulated."

"I wonder, Holmes, that even you can accommodate them in your mind."

"I have docketed them mentally in a number of different categories: the inessential; the intriguing; the significant; and the vital."

"I do not envy you your task."

"No more do I, Watson. It certainly has brought the occasional migraine. That is why I needed your company and our night out together: as a relief from this infernal avalanche of evidence and testimony. Come, we must be off in good time tomorrow. No doubt a hundred crimes will be committed in this great city tonight. Let us hope the hotel is secure and that we are not numbered among the dead by tomorrow."

With this disturbing salutation, Holmes went off to his room. Fortunately, the hotel was secure, and we survived the night.

12

Our train journey to Washington next morning was smooth and swift, even though the somewhat stark interior of Pennsylvania Station, a forbidding catacomb, was not designed to lift the spirits. Yet the new Amtrak cars sped over the rails and the journey was pleasant enough. Holmes had telephoned ahead in the usual way, and at Washington station we encountered the driver who had originally met us almost a week earlier at Dulles aerodrome. The limousine moved smoothly along Pennsylvania Avenue, past the White House, and proceeded to the leafy cul-de-sac in Georgetown, where our butler opened the door as we arrived. Holmes had hardly hung up his coat and deerstalker when he strode into the study leading off our sitting room. I heard his exclamation of pleasure within.

"Ah, good. All here, exactly as I had wished."

I joined him to see a long row of bound volumes, the roman numerals on the spines proceeding from I to XXVI. I knew at once what they represented: the twenty-six volumes of testimony and exhibits that Holmes had referred to so frequently during our peregrinations and discussions in the three cities we had visited that week. There were other materials besides, and I observed the green covers on volumes both thick and thin, relating to Hearings before committees of the United States Congress—some of them bearing on assassinations, others on intelligence agencies, as the covers declared. Holmes was already leafing through some of the Hearings, as if seeking clues to the problems confronting him. My curiosity must have shown itself, for he looked up, and surprised me with a low chuckle.

"You wonder why I am interested in what may appear dry documents from the laborious transcriptions of hearings before committees of the Congress, Watson. But there is excitement and interest here, I do declare. I have here the final reports of a select committee of the United States Congress looking into the activities of intelligence agencies during recent decades, and at the time of the assassination. Fabulous tales that put Professor Moriarty's exploits to shame. Here we have an unnamed character with the incognito "Amlash"—a high government official in Cuba willing to do diabolical deeds for the American intelligence agencies. Where, in all our many cases together, Watson, could we encounter such an improbable character? He was prepared to wield a poison pen dipped in some dreadful potion bringing instant death, the poison named 'Black Leaf 40'—an excellent name for a good tobacco, but not one of the shags I would recommend, Watson. Lethal, to say the least. And here," Holmes continued, seizing another volume of evidence, "here, Watson, a reference to the Chicago gangster Mr. Sam Giancana, who was killed on the eve of his appearance before this same committee of the Congress. Killed by whom, you may ask? These are dark waters, Watson. And here, in this volume, details of persons living in Miami hotels, acting at one and the same time for the CIA and for Mr. Howard Hughes, a Texas magnate, but with connections to the Mafiosi. I ask you, Watson, where in all our cases together did we encounter such a *galère?*"

"Amazing, Holmes. But does this not add to the complexities already confronting you? Where does it end, indeed where does it begin?" I gestured despairingly to the twenty-six dark blue volumes assembled on the desk between the ebony bookends, to the green progression of Hearings in soft covers on a shelf above, and what appeared to be even more materials in brown manila covers on the desk.

"Watson," declared Holmes, "somewhere, scattered in this vast jungle of words, there will be stray clues to what happened in Dealey Plaza on November 22, 1963. I confess that I do not expect to locate anything approaching a pattern to permit us to get beyond conjecture. But we must set our minds to such a task, whether or not it defeats us."

As he spoke, I remembered that Sherlock Holmes had been beaten four times in his career; three times by men, and once by a woman.

"I fear, Holmes, that this may well prove to be your fifth defeat."

"That may well be so, Watson. But I cannot think of a more honorable defeat, and I will retire contentedly with my violin and my microscope to write that little monograph on detection which I have put off these many years. But for the present, I remind myself once more of my observation in the *Boscombe Valley Mystery*—that detection is founded on the observation of trifles, and you will recall yourself what we agreed when we worked together on *The Speckled Band*—that insufficiency of data is the surest way to erroneous conclusions. I will go over these documents once again, after dinner."

At that, we went to our rooms. The butler had drawn a bath and I sank into the beneficent warmth of the tub to ease my limbs. At dinner, Holmes was in a mood I had learned to recognize from intimate association over many years. A slight flush lit those pale cheeks; the eyes glinted; the nostrils of that keen nose seemed to quiver with anticipation. It was the excitement of the chase. I was not a jot surprised when Holmes donned his smoking jacket immediately after dinner and excused himself to repair to the study. I agreed readily, and stated that I was ready for bed.

"Be good enough, Watson, to lend me your tobacco pouch. This is a three-pipe problem, and I am rather short of shag. Ah, the Arcadia mixture," he observed, as he sniffed the bag I threw him. "That should be good for concentration in the small hours. Goodnight, Watson." At which Holmes strode off to the study and closed the door. I retired immediately and was soon asleep.

I was accustomed to my old friend's habits of work, but I confess that I was taken aback when I came down to breakfast next morning to discover Holmes still ensconced in the study, his pipe laid aside. He was bent over the desk with a welter of volumes and papers about him—on the desk, on the floor, several tomes on the windowsill, and myriad pieces of paper sticking from the leaves of the books, adorned with curious hieroglyphs, no doubt indicating cross references and trails whose interconnections were locked within the sleuth's mind.

"Good morning, Watson." Holmes reached out to a volume from the long array before him. He handed it to me, his lean finger reaching into the leaves to locate the place he had marked. Two more volumes followed. "After breakfast, I would like you to study the drawings and photographs in these volumes, and then let us discuss them. Kindly draw on the results of your researches in New York City. They bear directly on a prime question."

I took the volumes and deposited them on the sideboard. After breakfast, a slight trace of weariness appeared on Holmes's features, but I knew my friend well enough to realize that he would make up his own mind on such matters as rest and recuperation after his long vigil. As a physician, I was relieved, however, at his announcement, after our breakfast toast and some excellent Cooper's Oxford marmalade our hosts had thoughtfully provided for us.

"I am now going to take a catnap, Watson, for an hour. Please rouse me if the clock should creep around to mid-morning. If you would be so good as to attend to my earlier request on your researches, we may have a fruitful discussion."

I expressed my relief that Holmes intended to rest, and took the volumes to my room. I perused them at a sidetable beneath a window giving out on to a gentle incline of grass and trees above the nearby Rock Creek Park. The bosky canyon subdued the murmur of traffic on the twin roads far beneath where I sat, so that I had an hour of undisturbed study and reflection. The principal objects of attention were drawings and representations created by an artist, on the instructions of physicians who had conducted the autopsy on the dead President at the Naval Hospital in nearby Bethesda. Holmes had scribbled notations on slips of paper, some of them cryptic inquiries, addressed to myself.

"Watson. Possible, probable, or improbable?" Or again, "Does the forensic evidence warrant the conclusion?"

My attention was drawn particularly to what appeared to be disparities between the accounts of the physicians attending the dying President at the Parkland Hospital in Dallas and those who began the autopsy later that day at Bethesda near Washington, D.C. As Holmes's notations indicated, the doctors at Dallas observed and reported on a massive head wound on the right side and rear portions of the President's skull. One physician in attendance referred to an entry wound at the temple. I drew on my notes and sketches from the archives at New York in order to study the somewhat different conclusions reached by the military doctors conducting the autopsy in Washington. By mid-morning I encountered some professional doubts—needless to say, with the necessary caveats dictated by a lack of direct evidence, most especially that of the cadaver itself.

Observing the hour, I tapped on Holmes's door. He came out almost at once, seemingly fully restored. I marveled again at that iron constitution. We descended to the study together, where Holmes cleared an arena of space on the desk and bade me draw up a chair. Together we pored over the volumes in question, with Holmes reaching out now and then for a volume of testimony from physicians who had appeared before the Warren Commission, and a further, more recent panel. Our discussion flowed to and fro, and Holmes darted many questions at me as his long fingers moved quickly from volume to volume. Two exhibits in particular had drawn his attention and he questioned me closely on the gruesome drawings produced by an artist to support a principal conclusion of the autopsy at the Washington hospital. They were numbered as "Commission Exhibit 386" and "388," and they showed the President leaning well forward in the Presidential car, his head sunk deeply on his chest, with a bullet entering the lower portion of the cranium at the rear, causing a neat hole well down in the occipito parietal region at the base of the palate, the bullet exiting at the top of the cranium and forward, taking away the top of the head.

"Your considered views on that, if you please, Watson," said Holmes. I surmised that my answer might be crucial in guiding his train of thought.

"My opinion, Holmes, is that the extensive skull damage shown there, affecting the major portion of the right cerebral hemisphere, accords with the observations made on the spot and contained in the main pathological report printed immediately alongside this drawing. Clearly, the pathologists encountered great difficulty in piecing together the evidence, not least because portions of the skull arrived later from Dallas, as separate specimens. But the main conclusion is that a missile entered the President's head from the rear, causing an entry point you observe here"—I drew attention once more to the drawing—"and exiting somewhere in this region here, the top right hand portion of the skull, carrying it away."

"But what difficulties do you find with that account, Watson?"

"I will admit, Holmes, that I find it difficult to conceive that a shot fired from a sixth-story window above the target should enter the rear lower portion of the skull and exit from the top. It appears to defy geometry, whether or not the President's head had slumped to such an extraordinary angle on his chest. On the latter point, the filmed and photographic evidence would not seem to confirm the drawing. Did I not read the testimony of some witnesses on the spot that the President was sitting bolt upright, clutching his neck, wounded by the first bullet to find its mark?"

"Correct, Watson. I am inclined to agree with you. You will note the photograph juxtaposed to this drawing, suggesting that the President finally slumped well over to his left, toward his wife. It is not possible that the fatal bullet came at that precise moment, given the trajectory. See here . . ." Holmes drew out a sketch he had made, showing angles of descent for the bullet—three possible angles in all. In each case, I found it difficult to link the angle with the clearly marked entry and exit points on the official exhibit.

Beyond these disagreements, further disagreements had arisen a good many years later, when a panel of experts looked again at the original autopsy reports. Among the documents Holmes handed me were freshly minted copies of recent Congressional Hearings on Assassinations, where the forensic evidence on the head wounds suffered by the President was reexamined, using new techniques based on what was termed "computerized simulation" of the President's skull. Illustrations relating to this simulation suggested that the fatal bullet exited on the upper right side of the head. The panel of experts who had reviewed the original autopsy reports had now concluded that the bullet entered the President's skull some four inches higher than as proposed by the original autopsy. The vital conclusion of this review of the evidence was that the bullet had entered the skull at the upper plate in the rear of the cranium, and exited at the right forward lobe. I found this conclusion difficult to accept as I looked at my own notes and drawings, and I conveyed my doubts to Holmes. Nevertheless, I felt it incumbent on me to put forward a defense of my colleagues in the profession.

"But surely, Holmes," I asseverated, "you cannot possibly believe that responsible pathologists would invent or even exaggerate their findings? That would represent a gross breach of medical ethics and . . ."

Holmes cut in quickly with his hand raised in admonishment.

"Not for one moment, Watson. In the pursuit of truth, we are concerned with evidence long before we attribute motives. Recall that all the pathologists involved have worked in conditions of extreme uncertainty. With such a massive wound, as you have already indicated, it would be hazardous in the extreme for anyone to claim certainty. I put another question to you, Watson. Did your researches in New York indicate that a bullet wound to the skull makes a clean entry—as we see here, where some portions of the skull were simply not available at the autopsy—with the major damage confined to the point of exit?" Holmes drew attention to another Warren Commission Exhibit—Number 400, again a drawing, of a somewhat facile simplicity, displaying a neat point of entry and massive injury at the point of exit, all in a horizontal plane.

"Impossible to say, Holmes, it depends on so many factors. Firstly, the bullet itself—its make and character, its shape and substance, its velocity—also the angle of entry and of course the point of entry. I am afraid this drawing strikes me as fanciful. In any case, the point of entry and angle of trajectory have no connection with the other impressions of the artists."

"We agree, Watson. A further difficulty is that the bullet which took away so much of the skull in this case was never confirmed. So the physicians could not establish anything from retrieval of the bullet. Some minute portions of metal were found embedded in the skull, but not sufficient to match them to any particular bullet or weapon, according to the original reports of the ballistics experts."

"What of the more recent findings, Holmes—from the panel of specialists assisting the Congressional committee?"

"They concluded that the minute fragments found in the President's skull matched ammunition attributed to Oswald's rifle."

"That must conclude the matter, surely?"

"Not quite, Watson. We would have to know the exact provenance of the minute fragments sent out for independent analysis—how and where they were originally found, where they were stored—whether by the FBI, or in some independent archive from the outset. Indeed, there are a number of steps intervening, not least the intervention of a decade and a half between the original autopsy and the latest conclusions."

"What other doubts persist in your mind, Holmes?"

"The matter of the magic bullet—the one that is reputed to have passed through the President's neck, through Governor Connally at several points in his body, to emerge intact on one of the two stretchers that carried the President and the Governor into Parkland Hospital in Dallas. No one is sure upon which stretcher it was found. And we will agree, Watson, it was clearly not that bullet which caused this massive head wound."

"Quite impossible, Holmes. At the very least, it would be flattened at the head, but more likely it would have disintegrated. The skull is an extremely tough and resilient structure, as you no doubt know, fashioned by millions of years of natural selection."

"We have already discussed the characteristics of missiles that fracture on impact, causing massive damage at the point of entry. If something of that character had been fired from the right front, would that be commensurate with the effects we have noted, Watson?"

"In my opinion it would, Holmes."

"I see. Is there anything else you observe about the drawing here, Watson?"

I looked again. I could see nothing beyond the grisly testimony to the dreadful tragedy it represented.

"Here, take my glass." Holmes handed me his magnifying glass. Looking again, I saw, magnified several times, the minute lettering of an artist's inscription, no doubt much larger on the original, much smaller here.

"I see the artist's initials. And a date. It appears to be 3/64. I imagine that must be March, 1964, the date of the drawing."

"Four months after the autopsy, Watson. A small point, perhaps, but we must note it."

"But the pathologist's initial notes and sketches are extant, are they not?"

"The pathologist at the Naval Hospital in Bethesda destroyed his original notes."

"Good heavens! That I did not know. He surely appreciated that they comprised historic documents of the utmost importance?"

"You would know better than I can, Watson, what prompts a medical specialist to destroy his notes on any particular occasion. I am myself very surprised, but it is not for us to conjure reasons. One cannot entertain doubts of good faith. The volumes here contain the physician's testimony. It was perhaps a trifle unfortunate that Commander Humes, the specialist at the Naval Hospital at that particular hour on Friday night, could claim expertise in the treatment of natural diseases, but not, alas, in the pathology of violent wounds—as the Commander personally testified. That is why he called in a colleague, Colonel Finck, an expert in the field of wound ballistics, to assist him. It was Dr. Finck who introduced into the official transcripts the drawings we have been studying."

"But the volume from the Warren Commission that you passed to me this morning—Volume 17—contains Commander Humes's written notes at the conclusion of the autopsy. That is the best available evidence, surely?"

"Observe, Watson, the date of the Commander's notes." I detected in my companion's voice a chiding note. "In his initial testimony, the Commander said that his report, with its conclusions, was developed and completed some 24 to 48 hours after the President's death. The second page of his written report states that on Saturday, November 23, the day following the President's death and the morning after the autopsy, the Commander telephoned the physicians at Dallas concerning the amount of inspection carried out on the body before it was sent to Washington. This dates the notes after Saturday morning. On pages 8 and 9 of the physician's notes, he refers to three fragments of skull received separately from Dallas—those retrieved from

Elm Street, it seems, and sent on later—that corresponded approximately to the dimensions of the large injury to the skull. The largest portion of skull is said to contain what is presumably—that was Commander Humes's term—a roughly circular wound of exit, estimated to measure some 2.5 to 3.0 centimeters in diameter. These details do not appear to fit the drawing done some months later by the artist, under instruction. Again, in Colonel Humes's notes on that original weekend, there are revisions and modifications on the page. And note here, Watson, at page 14, The fatal missile entered the skull above and to the right of the external occipital protuberance. That description does not quite tally with the drawings we have been examining. The Commander's rough drawings that weekend would also seem to indicate severe injury in the area of the right eye."

I looked again at the autopsy drawings in Exhibit 397 which Holmes held before me.

"The Commander handed over his notes and working papers to the Commanding Officer of the Naval Medical School at 5 o'clock on Sunday, November 24. At the same time he affirmed in writing that he had burned certain preliminary draft notes relating to the official autopsy report. Oswald was killed that same Sunday morning, before noon."

"What, then, do you conclude from all this, Holmes?"

"Nothing venal, Watson. No question of that. Uncertainty, perhaps. Bear in mind that the whole weight of the world's press and television throughout that weekend pointed to a lone assassin shooting from a lair six floors up, to the rear of the President. It would be a brave medical specialist who wrote a report—or any part of a

—157

report—proposing a different direction, another assassin. I also remain puzzled, Watson, by the combined weight of the testimony from the Dallas hospital that the President had a massive wound in the rear portion of the skull. Dr. Robert McClelland was stationed immediately behind the President's head as he lay dying in the trauma room, and he was able to observe the injury more closely perhaps than any of his colleagues present, as his testimony makes clear. In writing his report at 4:45 P.M. that same day, he stated that the cause of death was massive head and brain injury from a gunshot wound to the left temple. Dr. Perry, the senior pathologist in attendance at the Dallas hospital, testified that when the President arrived in the trauma room he observed a large avulsive wound on the right posterior cranium. Not, you observe, Watson, at the top of the President's head. At an understandably confused meeting with the press soon after the President was pronounced dead, Dr. Perry was asked if one bullet could have struck the President from the front. He affirmed that this was conceivable. It is worth noting that the physicians at that hour at the Parkland Hospital in Dallas were not apprised of any evidence suggesting that all the shots came from the rear, and from above. The pathologists were simply reporting on what their professional training allowed them to see in the trauma room as the President died.

"Note, too, the testimony of Dr. Jenkins, who attended the President at Dallas and the testimony of the other surgeons and pathologists that day—eight or more— who assisted in the various tasks of surgery and attempts at resuscitation. Those who observed the head wounds confirm that the main injury appeared toward the rear of the skull. In short, the rear portion of the President's head was blown off. That is what puzzles me, Watson. It was unfortunate that, when the Warren Commission held its hearings, the Dallas physicians were invited to give their testimony to the Commission *after* the testimony of the Commanders who conducted the autopsy at Washington. Logic required that the Commission's lawyers should have commenced with expert witnesses at the Dallas hospital, especially in view of the major tracheotomy obliterating the neck wound, performed at Dallas in the attempt to save the President's life. When the corpse arrived in Washington, a considerable amount of surgery had already been performed. As the volumes of evidence make plain, the lawyers putting questions to the Dallas physicians clearly took their cues from the results of the Washington autopsy, having listened to the testimony of the Washington physicians first. The logic of that procedure escapes me, I confess."

"It hardly squares with correct forensic procedures, not to mention logic. I am with you there, Holmes. But Holmes," I continued, "how do you account for the fact that these same Dallas physicians accepted the results of the autopsy performed later at the Bethesda hospital without so much as a murmur?"

"I think you know better than I do, Watson, that in the medical profession, especially in forensics, colleagues are most reluctant to contradict each other. To do so is to risk a professional slur. The military doctors conducting the autopsy at Bethesda had the last word, and their colleagues in Dallas had to presume a much more detailed inspection in Washington than the emergency surgery at Dallas could possibly provide, in conditions that were far short of ideal. Note, too, that a supplementary autopsy report was prepared two weeks after the first autopsy report. This shows the elements of uncertainty present.

"Given the massive nature of the wound, the doctors in Washington had to reconstruct as best they could, and for a time they lacked portions of the President's skull, as you know. Throughout that weekend, the weight of evidence from official sources placed all the shots with a lone assassin firing from the rear, and above the level of the street. Physicians listen to radio and television too, Watson. To conjure a wound with a frontal entry would have entailed challenging the official orthodoxy already in spate in the media. An element of uncertainty was clearly present at Washington when Commander Humes telephoned his Dallas colleagues on Saturday morning. He wrote up his report on the following day, Sunday. An unenviable task. The second autopsy report two weeks later is a worrisome factor. It is a very great pity that the Commander burned his notes for the first autopsy report. To repeat, there is no doubting the physician's probity: the question at issue is whether there were degrees of uncertainty between Friday and Sunday that were finally resolved in favor of a report asserting that shots came only from the rear."

"But were there not others present at the autopsy in Washington who could have expressed doubts?"

"Commander Humes and Colonel Finck, the army physician, conducted the autopsy. Others assisted, including Commander Boswell, but the Commander, the only additional physician called to testify, was merely asked if he supported Commander Humes's autopsy report, which he did, and whether he wished to add to or modify any part of it. He did not."

"Do I not recall from some source, Holmes, that other

observers were present during the examination?"

"Correct, Watson. Members of the Secret Service were present, including Special Agent Mr. Kellerman, who was in the Presidential car when the shots were fired, in the front seat next to the driver, with immediate responsibility for protecting the President. Mr. Kellerman's observations on the autopsy were of course those of a layman without medical qualifications. He could only testify to what he saw or heard at the Bethesda hospital, where he was present after accompanying the corpse back to Washington."

"Did he make any observations?"

"He remarked to the Commission that, to his knowledge, only one fragment of bullet was removed from the President's head during the autopsy—it was removed from inside and above the right eye."

"Do you then conclude that the trajectory of the bullet through the head started at that point, or ended there?"

"I conclude neither, since it is impossible to say, on the basis of the evidence. However, Counsel did put some earlier questions to Mr. Kellerman on the events in Dealey Plaza at the moment the President was shot. Kellerman said that a flurry of shells came into the car. By the time he testified, in March of 1964, Mr. Kellerman had been given the opportunity to view the Zapruder film of the assassination. He clearly persisted in his belief that more than three shots were fired—in a quick flurry. Then he observed to Counsel that if they would view the film, they might come up with an answer different to the one they plainly wished to adopt."

"Meaning a different hypothesis to that of shots from the rear only?"

"Alas, that is not clear from the testimony or the ques-

—161

tions directed at the witness. The remark was simply not followed up. It is one of the more unsatisfactory aspects of the volumes we have here, Watson, that so many questions were not asked, so many vital leads not followed up. Regrettably, the proceedings of the recent Congressional investigation were evidently guided, though not dictated, by the single assassin theory, since they had no time to explore the inconsistencies between testimony presented only recently to the Congressmen and that given earlier to the Warren Commission. For instance, in the evidence presented to the Warren Commission, police officer Weitzman, who was on the spot, testifies that he found portions of the President's skull on the street, which he retrieved, and these were sent on later to the pathologists who had conducted the autopsy at the Washington hospital. In one part of the testimony to the Congressional committee, following a detailed reconsideration by pathologists, it was stated that portions of the President's skull they examined were found in the Presidential car. The two sets of statements do not match. Again, the forensic experts were not able to identify an entry point at the back of the skull, because of the massive damage and the fracturing effect. Yet they asserted that the entry point was four inches higher than that indicated by Commander Humes and his colleagues who performed the original autopsy. Despite these difficulties, the panel reporting to the Congressional Committee concluded that perforation of the skull must have come from the rear, nowhere else."

"And do you share that conclusion, Holmes?"

"I do not accept it, and I do not discount it. My own observations at Washington, coupled with your own researches, impel me to accept as a possibility, at the least, a bullet fired from immediately to the right, and forward of the car, from the area of the grassy knoll. I couple with this the clear photographic evidence that Mrs. Kennedy's instant reaction was to attempt to clamber over the rear of the Presidential limousine. Whether this was to attempt to retrieve portions of her husband's skull, or to escape from the line of fire in a car moving very slowly, at no more than ten miles an hour, I do not know. But we do know that police motorcyclists to the rear of the limousine were sprayed with blood and brain tissue; and that Mr. Zapruder, who filmed the moment of the assassination from the knoll, testified that a shot came from behind him; and that a great many witnesses, including police officer Weitzman, ran immediately up the grassy knoll, from which direction they had heard at least one shot, while some saw a puff of smoke, and some smelled the odor of cordite immediately in that area.

"But we have talked long enough, Watson. I wish to get back to my notes. I suggest you take the air in the nation's capital, and we will resume our discussion later."

At this, Holmes vanished to the study and silence fell upon the house.

_____13

I devoted the afternoon to a leisurely inspection of the natural history sections of the Smithsonian Institution. When I returned in the early evening, I discovered that Holmes had spread upon the floor of the study a number of drawings, showing possible trajectories of bullets fired from different directions. After a preliminary greeting, he went back to his task, moving the drawings about the floor, and bending over them with a rule and a set square he had obtained from some source. Anon he joined me in the sitting room.

"How many bullets would you say were fired in Dealey Plaza that day, Watson?" he began. I thought carefully.

"At least three."

Holmes chuckled briefly. "Agreed, Watson. At least three, possibly four. As you may know, fresh evidence came to light recently from a police broadcasting radio switched on at the time of the assassination, which would seem to confirm four shots—after due allowance for any echo effects. Our question is, what happened to the fourth bullet? And the fourth cartridge case? Only three were found in the Book Depository, and none in the breech of the rifle discovered there. A curious aspect of the original investigations was the neatness and completeness of the case against Oswald in this regard. Three cartridge shells were found next to the open window on the sixth floor. The President was clearly observed by onlookers to be hit twice, at the least, and Governor Connally was also observed to be hit. Later, at the Parkland Hospital, the so-called magic bullet was found on one of the stretchers in pristine condition. This bullet was later found to match Oswald's rifle, though it remains a quite remarkable feat that it passed through the President's neck, traveled on to wound Governor Connally in the back, and then in the wrist and thigh, presumably to fall out on to the floor of the Presidential car in its forward trajectory. But how this same intact bullet performed all this and then found its way separately on to a stretcher, or otherwise fell out of Governor Connally's thigh or wrist, remains a central mystery, which is certainly not cleared up by the recent Congressional investigation. Moreover, the fact that a bullet is later found which matches a particular firearm is not proof that it was discharged by that same firearm on any particular day, or occasion.''

"But surely, Holmes,'' I put in, "the bullets and any fragments were handed over to the authorities on the spot that same day, together with the cases. If memory serves from my reading of the Warren Commission Report, they were all promptly handed over to the FBI and sent on to Washington for inspection.''

"Not quite, Watson. You were not able to read the volumes of evidence attached to the main Report, but you will find in Volume 3, page 414, if memory serves, that two cartridge cases were received at the FBI laboratories in Washington, D.C., on November 23, 1963. The third was received some days later—on November 27, in fact. It was delivered by Special Agent Vincent Drain, of the Dallas office, and by Special Agent Warren De Brueys."

"De Brueys?" I queried. "He of the New Orleans office that same summer—the one you discussed earlier?"

"The same. The agent who omitted to file an affidavit with Mr. J. Edgar Hoover's generous but incomplete renderings to the Commission in 1964."

"What could explain the delay in sending the third cartridge? And what of a fourth one, Holmes?"

"An explanation is not available, so we cannot know."

"But Holmes," I put in, "the recent independent investigation of the ballistic evidence, carried out for the committee of the Congress, confirmed that all the bullet fragments found in the two victims, and all fragments found in the Presidential car, came from only two bullets —the one that is said to have wounded the President and Governor Connally, and the bullet that shattered the President's skull."

"We would need to know the exact provenance of the fragments sent to any independent analyst before we drew any firm conclusions, Watson."

"I do not follow you, Holmes."

"Bear in mind that testing techniques were applied to the same fragments by the FBI, using all their technical and laboratory skills, in 1964. The results were inconclusive, and the FBI therefore abstained from reporting them. After a lapse of more than twelve years, fragments were sent to a nuclear chemist at the University of California for tests, using newly developed techniques termed 'neutron activation analysis.' I will spare you the technical details, Watson, but they are most impressive."

"So no doubt remains, Holmes? We cannot doubt the

word of an independent university chemist, surely?"

"There is a prior question. Did some of the fragments provided to the chemist come from the Presidential car, and some from within the President's skull? Was this established independently of the FBI? If not, the tests were of very limited value. They would merely confirm what is not at issue—namely, that at least one shot, and most probably two, but possibly three shots were fired at the occupants of the Presidential car from a rifle identified with Lee Harvey Oswald. The ballistic evidence does not go beyond that, in the absence of any precise and indubitable evidence concerning the original retrieval and subsequent storage of the fragments.

"Moreover, the recent findings throw no light on what happened to the other bullet, or two bullets, if we rely on the police radio, which recorded four shots. One of those shots may have been the stray bullet that damaged the pavement at a point well above and beyond a direct line of fire into the limousine. If Oswald had such deadly accuracy with only two shots at the limousine, why did he send a third, wild shot so wide of the mark? The trajectories make it impossible to account for the shot by means of a ricochet from the victims of the attack, or from the Presidential car. Why, then, did Oswald—if it was he—fire so wide? If it was the first shot he fired, he was disastrously limiting any possibility of finding his target with the second—and many expert commentators continue to have doubts on the time factor even for two shots aimed directly at the limousine. If four shots were recorded—the flurry reported by Mr. Roy Kellerman, a man professionally trained over a great many years as the President's chief bodyguard to record just such evidence —the mystery deepens further.

"Recall, Watson, the recently released reports of the Congressional committee, where Governor Connally and his wife testified with the utmost conviction that it was the second shot that hit the Governor. Both the Governor and Mrs. Connally are entirely certain that they heard the first shot, and that it was a second shot that hit the Governor. In the Governor's words, 'I *heard* the first shot. I *felt* the second one.' Governor Connally went on to say that he heard only two shots, and that both came from the rear. However, the shot that hit him drove him forward, so that he slumped on to his wife's lap. In such a position, it would be difficult for any person to know the direction of any subsequent shots, and a great deal of noise was already erupting in the Plaza, as soon as the first and second shots were fired. Mrs. Connally remains convinced that she heard three shots. This accords with the testimony of scores of other witnesses. Was the third shot fired at the pavement well beyond the car? If so, why? It could only delay the flight of the assassin, unless it was designed to serve some other purpose."

"Have you conjured other reasons, Holmes?"

"My exercises with ruler and set square today clearly suggested that the bullet which damaged the pavement could only have come from one direction—the sixth floor of the Book Depository. Our hypotheses must start from there. Did Oswald—or whoever fired that shot—intend to draw attention away from another gunman? To be more fanciful—but within the realms of possibility, as an early conjecture suggested to me—was Oswald deliberately firing a shot above the President's head in order to warn him of the dangers he was courting by riding in an open limousine in a city given to much violence? Was

Oswald duped into what he thought was a special commission, for the Secret Service, say, in order to bring something home to the President, in his own best interests? If so, was Oswald deluded, and when the full horror of what occurred in Dealey Plaza came to him only later, did this—indeed, did it not—account adequately for all his movements and his behavior thereafter?"

We sat in silence for some moments as the extraordinary import of what Holmes had said registered in my mind. I could not contain my question.

"Holmes, what is your opinion? Have you made any deductions?"

Holmes stood up in silence and strode to the window. He stared out for what seemed an eternity.

"No firm deductions, Watson. There is not sufficient evidence. What is available is cold, very cold. So many of the crucial witnesses are dead, most notably Mr. Jack Ruby. He died of cancer, so let us not indulge conspiracy theories there. Or let us hope not. Yet his behavior throughout that infamous weekend, and then later as a terrified witness before the Warren Commission—a man clearly in deep fear for his life from sinister forces, as he himself blurted out—casts very dark shadows over this case."

I felt it might help Holmes if I prompted him to review the strange events surrounding Mr. Jack Ruby at the time of the assassination, and I encouraged my companion to go over them. I was glad he assented.

"I need not expand on the seedy way of life Mr. Jack Ruby maintained, as the owner of two night clubs in Dallas. They were frequented by a mixture of clientele, from rich oil men with a taste for feminine company, to Dallas police officers, to visitors from out of town—from other parts of Texas, from New Orleans, from Chicago even, where Ruby grew up and where he had associations in the darker hinterland of American society.

"On the day the President died, Mr. Jack Ruby was extremely active, and his presence was observed in several locations linked with the infamous events of that day. Photographic evidence is sometimes reliable, sometimes not, as you know, Watson. But if we begin in Dealey Plaza, minutes after the President was shot, one photograph taken on the spot shows a distinct likeness of Mr. Ruby in a small crowd standing on the steps of the Book Depository. That could be innocent enough, and it is printed in the Warren Report, but unhappily the photo appears to have been cropped at just the point where Ruby—if indeed it was Ruby—was standing, so that he is only half visible.

"What is indubitable is that Ruby turned up at the Parkland Hospital as the President lay dying. There is expert and reliable testimony to that from quite different sources, including those who knew Ruby and talked with him there. Later that day, it is fairly clear that Ruby was seen again in the area where the President was killed. He was also at the Police Department until a late hour on Friday night, and again on Saturday. Finally, on Sunday he walked, apparently unseen, through a tight police cordon at the Dallas police headquarters in order to shoot Oswald in front of armed members of the law enforcement agencies. This, mark you, after anonymous telephone calls to police headquarters during the weekend declaring that if and when Oswald was moved, he was going to be killed."

"But do I not recall, Holmes, that Ruby spent some minutes at a Western Union office sending a check to an employee, facts later corroborated, just shortly before shooting Oswald? That hardly suggests a carefully arranged plan? He could not know how long his business at the Western Union office would take."

"You are right to raise the question, Watson. Others have done so. But men who have agreed to commit dastardly acts very often devote the time before the deed to pursuits that take their mind off what they intend to do, or what they know they must do, whether under instructions, or threats, or by inducement—it matters little. Again, you must bear in mind that the transfer of Oswald from the Dallas Police Department that weekend was delayed more than once, and inexplicably, for considerable lengths of time. A number of explanations could be offered, but among them we must at least consider that Ruby had not yet signalled a required response. We still do not know how he entered the basement of the police station without being seen, even though he was a very familiar figure there, as the police themselves, and numerous other witnesses, attested. One curious strand of evidence is that a Police Lieutenant on the force, Mr. Jack Revill, testified that at 9:30 on that Sunday morning, Ruby went up in the elevator at police headquarters to the third floor, where the offices of the police officials and the interrogation rooms were located. Lieutenant Revill said that Ruby rode up the elevator with a Baptist minister named Rushing, who had come wishing to offer spiritual guidance to Oswald."

"And no doubt the pastor confirmed this?"

"The pastor was not called to testify."

"But this is astounding, Holmes. You declare that a Baptist minister, presumably known to many in the area, possessing vital evidence on Ruby's movements before he shot Oswald, was not called to testify, among some 500 other witnesses summoned?''

"I fear not, Watson. If I were to list the witnesses not summoned for vital portions of the train of events that weekend, we should be here for some time yet. But no doubt you appreciate somewhat better the problems I have encountered here. Unknown to you, Watson, I attempted to contact sundry persons in the cities we have visited this past week, although there was an acute problem of withholding my identity. The one or two I was able to contact were either struck with fear, or had firmly decided not to speak to anyone on any account, despite —or possibly because of—the lapse of time. Naturally I did not and could not press the matter.''

"So there are still loose ends, Holmes?''

"A great many. For example, in 1964, two very experienced salesmen in a gun shop in Irving, near Dallas, testified that a repair tag was issued to a Mr. Oswald in the first part of November 1963. It related to fixing a telescopic sight on a rifle. Yet the rifle Oswald was held to have used was already fitted with that device. Despite elaborate checks, no other person by the name of Oswald was traced in the vicinity, and the evidence of the two salesmen—one of them the owner of the shop—was compelling. Other shop owners and employees nearby confirmed a visit by Oswald—or if not, by someone very much like him—some time before the assassination. The Commission dismissed all this evidence, on the grounds that if Oswald used his alias, Hidell, for the purchase of the other two weapons associated with him, there was no good reason for him to use his own proper name for a further transaction involving another weapon.''

—172

"Unless he felt he had nothing to fear on this occasion?"

"Or was it, again, someone posing as Oswald? The Commission's second reason for dismissing the testimony was that the police were led to the shop by an anonymous telephone call made soon after Oswald's death, referring to the work on the gun and giving details of the shop where the repair was carried out. We are left with another mystery, because that unusual piece of information proved correct. Who would have known?"

"But was there time for an Oswald, or any accomplice —indeed for anyone in Dallas—to plot to kill the President during his visit? When was the visit confirmed, Holmes?"

"By mid-September the Dallas newspapers had confirmed the visit of President Kennedy to Texas. By September 26, it was further announced that the visit would be on November 21 and 22, and that Dallas would be included in the itinerary. On October 14, Oswald moved his address in Dallas from one rooming house to another, where he now rented a room under the assumed name of O.H. Lee. On November 1, Oswald rented a post box at the Terminal Annex Post Office in Dallas, near the Book Depository. A curious form of extra expense for an impecunious man. On November 7, Ruby rented a post box in the same post office for the period up to December 31, 1964, the box a matter of a few feet away from Oswald's box. Ruby's was entered as a letter drop for a business venture named Earl Products.

"And what could be the significance of this, Holmes?"

"It *could* be—I do not say that this occurred—that Ruby was thus able to communicate with Oswald at short notice, without an intermediary, if that should prove necessary, and without meeting."

"I think I catch your drift. Pray go on."

"Early in November, as we have noted before, Oswald showed interest in buying a car, declaring to car salesmen—one of whom wrote down Oswald's name—that he, Oswald, had some money coming in soon. At the same time, Oswald was requesting Mrs. Ruth Paine to give him driving lessons. This she did, using her own car."

"That was surely unsurprising, for a young man in Texas? Indeed, it was surprising that Oswald was not already driving a car."

"Agreed. The question was, where would the money come from? Not from his place of employment, certainly. His pay was niggardly in the extreme. He could not afford to maintain his wife and child. Another child had already arrived, on October 20. Oswald had moved to a rooming house where he had a single room costing eight dollars a week."

"You are suggesting, Holmes, that Oswald may have accepted a proposition from someone—possibly from Ruby?"

"A man in Oswald's dire straits *could* have accepted a proposition from almost any quarter at that time, given his personal circumstances, given that he could see no future for himself, and given that the last shreds of his belief in any economic or political system had already disintegrated."

"Do you have any further items in this concatenation of events?"

"If we move forward to the day of the assassination, Oswald's movements between 12:30 P.M. and about 1:30

P.M. are not entirely accounted for, except that Mrs. Roberts, the housekeeper at the rooming house, observed him to enter about 1:00 and to leave hurriedly within a few minutes—the time at which, in her testimony, she claimed to hear a police car sound its horn outside. Oswald left the house in a direction that lay in the vicinity of Mr. Jack Ruby's apartment. Mr. Ruby's complete movements after 12:30 that Friday are also unaccounted for, apart from the witnesses at Parkland Hospital. He declined to give an explanation of his movements when he testified before the Commission."

"But we do know, Holmes, that he was in a state of considerable alarm."

"Indeed we do, Watson. As though a plan had miscarried, perhaps."

A thought suddenly occurred to me. "Holmes!" I exclaimed. "Was it possible that Patrolman Tippit brought his car to Oswald's rooming house, gave a signal, and at another location informed Oswald that a plan had miscarried in some way?"

"That could certainly fit the pattern of events we have traced, Watson. It could also help to explain Tippit's death on the spot, if he was also involved. If Oswald had been hired to provide decoy shots, or merely warning shots, and if Oswald then had reason to believe that he was being tied into a murder that he did not commit, his actions thereafter would certainly fit that explanation of events. If he had agreed to kill the President, on the other hand, and payment was withheld, we could expect an equally drastic turn of events that afternoon. It would further explain why someone would have to eliminate Oswald before he could talk to anyone. Perhaps he was meant to be eliminated when he was at large in Dallas that weekend. His arrest in a cinema resulted unexpectedly, when an ordinary citizen happened to see him dive in there, in a sudden, suspicious manner. That complicated any intention to do away with Oswald. Once he was in the hands of the law, they were responsible for his safety. No policeman could risk killing Oswald. This prize was much too big for that."

At this point, Holmes broke off the discussion.

"Now, Watson, the clock advances. I have some further notes to make, and I suggest an early night. I give my report to our clients tomorrow morning, and by mid-afternoon I expect us to be airborne for London."

The butler appeared at the door, announcing dinner, and we turned to lighter topics, in a mood of reminiscence, as we dined quietly. Even so, I could observe that one part of Holmes's formidable mental apparatus was returning, inwardly and privately, to the matter in hand, and I was not surprised when he excused himself from a postprandial to return to the study. I read a book for a while, then retired to bed. I knew that at times like this, Holmes could summon up prodigious reserves of energy to work far into the night. Even so, I was genuinely concerned for my oldest companion and staunchest friend. He would be happy indeed to retire to his place in Sussex after this exhausting odyssey.

14

Soon after breakfast next morning, we packed our few belongings, thanked the good people who had looked after us so well, and handed our luggage to the chauffeur who called at the appointed time. It was but a short distance to the larger house where we were bound, and Holmes elected to walk. The car would follow later.

The air was cool, and Holmes stepped briskly over the leaves bestrewing the road. We reached the large house in a matter of minutes. Holmes handed his Inverness and deerstalker to the footman, who took my overcoat and hat in turn. We ascended the staircase and came into the room that we had encountered only a week ago.

Before us the same group of people was assembled, though with one or two additional ones, all gathered about the broad fireplace in the long salon. I should be guilty of an indiscretion if I were even to hint at the identities of those I saw before me now. Suffice to say that their names and faces were known well beyond the borders of the American Republic. The gentlemen, who stood on our arrival, disposed themselves about the settees and chaises longues. The lady, who I now knew to be our chief client, addressed herself to Sherlock Holmes.

"Mr. Holmes, we know only too well the dimensions of the problem we placed before you: we have wrestled with it for many years ourselves, with professional assistance and advice. We turned to you because we were baffled. We ask no more than that you give us your thoughts. No one is expecting a miracle. We know that the whole truth cannot be gained at this late time. But we ask you to be frank with us."

"Very well, ma'am," said Holmes. "I concur that this is a baffling case—more complex by far than any I have ever encountered in a career that spans a good many years. I can do no more, perhaps, than throw some particles of light in dark corners. My method, as you may know, ma'am, and gentlemen, is to proceed by logical analysis, using deductive methods on the whole, but with an eye and an ear for what I term unconsidered trifles, which often prove to be of much greater moment, when placed in a pattern, than their separate, unconsidered existence initially suggests. With such a vast array of circumstance in this case, my methods have been very sorely tried. But enough of these preambles. I will come straight to the point, as I know you prefer. I will then set out what few deductions seem plausible after such a lapse of years.

"The official Report of the Warren Commission concluded that the President was assassinated by Lee Harvey Oswald, acting alone and without accomplices, and that Oswald was not involved in any conspiracy with others to kill the President. The Commission found further that there was no evidence to support any speculation that Oswald was an agent, employee, or informant of any governmental agency in the United States, or the agent of any foreign power. More recently, a Committee of the Congress has concluded an intensive investigation, with expert witnesses, in an attempt to reassess the main conclusions of the original inquiry of 1964. The Congressional Committee accepts the conclusions of the 1964 Report, with some few caveats on a possible conspiracy.

"My own chief conclusions, ma'am, gentlemen, is that Oswald did not act alone. I think that others were involved in the killing of the President. I do not know who, or how many there were. When I observe that, in my belief, Oswald did not act alone, I do not mean by this that Oswald did not fire a rifle at the President from the sixth floor of the Texas School Book Depository at the time of the President's death. On balance, I believe that he did, but I have not found any evidence to confirm indubitably that he fired at the President to kill, or to wound him. I have found a great deal of persuasive conjecture that he did so, much circumstantial evidence to support those conjectures, but none that could not be demolished before an impartial tribunal or in a court of law, applying the rules of evidence.

"Lacking proof positive, I have myself been forced back on conjecture, drawing on a multitude of clues and a great many leads pointing in different directions, some of them mutually exclusive. To relate even a portion of them would detain us here for the rest of today, and I take as my principal task a brief review of possible—though I do not say probable—explanations of the crime, ending with some recommendations. I must stress, however, that I do not see it as any part of my task to instruct the citizens of this Republic in matters that are their own province, and you would very properly reject with contumely any presumption on my part that I should do so. I am a guest in your country, and your affairs of state are your own.

"Let us start with known and indubitable facts. The President was killed by rifle fire in Dealey Plaza, at Dallas in Texas, on November 22, 1963. Governor Connally of Texas, riding in the same Presidential car, was wounded by gunshot at the same time. The overwhelming testimony of many scores of witnesses in or near to Dealey Plaza at that time confirms that at least three shots were fired; some said four shots were fired, and some said more. After due allowance for possible echo effects in that partly enclosed plaza, and bearing in mind the many witnesses who were on the spot, particularly the number of witnesses at some little distance from the plaza who observed, quite independently, that the second and third shots were very close together, I conclude that the order of shots fired was thus. A first shot, the lapse of perhaps two or three seconds, then a second shot, and then, almost instantly, a third shot. It is my view that a fourth shot was fired, but by then the overwhelming majority of witnesses in Dealey Plaza were in a state of confusion, shock, and a degree of terror, so that their minds were blocked out by considerations for their own safety and for those with them, or about them.

"The President was seen by many witnesses to clutch his throat at the time a shot was first heard. There is also ample evidence from those in the car with him that he exclaimed at that instant that he had been hit. That wound was almost certainly near his neck, entering at his back. There was then a pause and two further shots followed. The President was mortally wounded in the head, possibly by a second bullet, but also possibly by a third. At least two shots came from the rear of the car at an angle that corresponded to a trajectory from the sixth floor of the Texas School Book Depository, to the right rear of the open car. Some witnesses attested that they had observed a man with a rifle at a particular window on the sixth floor shortly before the assassination, and many more claimed that they heard shots from that direction at the moment of the assassination. The wounds inflicted on Governor Connally, together with at least one of the wounds inflicted on the President, make it quite certain that shots were fired at the Presidential car from that direction. It is possible that shots were also fired from another location to the rear of the car, but there is no firm body of evidence to support such a surmise. It is extremely doubtful that any such secondary source of shots could be established beyond the realm of mere surmise at this date, not least because of a lack of evidence now on the character of the wounds suffered by the President and by Governor Connally.

"It is my firm belief that at least one shot was fired at the President from the area of the tree-covered grassy knoll that was to the front and to the right of the President's car as it descended Elm Street toward the triple underpass carrying overhead railroad lines. The evidence supporting this derives chiefly from the immediate actions of scores of people as the shots were fired and from the testimony of a majority of the witnesses who were interviewed within hours of the assassination, as well as those interviewed that weekend, and those who gave testimony to the Commission in the weeks and months that followed. Those witnesses included people from all walks of life who were stationed at all points around the plaza, on top of the overpass, inside the

School Book Depository, in open vehicles before and behind the Presidential limousine, and on foot—some of them ordinary citizens, others members of the Secret Service or police officers. To trace through the independent testimonies of these scores of witnesses scattered, alas, in several volumes of evidence to the Warren Commission, is to arrive at the conclusion that at least one shot was fired from an area hidden by a long wooden fence, beneath trees, giving a direct, uninterrupted view of the President at short range as he sat in the open car. The short range, the trajectory, and the very slow speed of the car made the President an easy target for a marksman armed with a rifle using a telescopic sight. In my opinion, the fatal wound that blew away the top rear portions of the President's head almost certainly came from the grassy knoll. I cannot offer you proof positive for this judgment.

"I also believe it was the third shot that inflicted the fatal wound. I think it probable that the second shot coming from the rear struck Governor Connally in the back, the bullet tumbling forward to strike his wrist and thigh.

"My conclusions are drawn in part from a consideration of the wounds, especially those to the President's head, to the extent that I have been permitted observation and inspection, though I must declare that this was not at first hand, nor as detailed as I would have desired. Detailed consideration and inspection is denied to the investigator by the strictures imposed at the National Archives and by considerations of taste. I must add, of course, that other strands of evidence have impelled me to my beliefs, not merely the testimony of so many witnesses on the spot, but also the photographic evidence

—some of it published, and other evidence retained in the Archives. I also add to this evidence other factors relating to the imperfect weapon believed to have discharged three shots in a few seconds at a distant, moving target, at least two shots with deadly accuracy, from a difficult firing position, with a difficult, falling trajectory. None of us would claim expertise on the laws of chance, but my own estimation is that the received, official version places too much credence on an astonishing array of ballistical chance."

At this point, one of the gentlemen sitting on a chaise longue leaned forward to interrupt Holmes. I had noticed that he showed slight signs of excitation as Holmes continued with his statement.

"Excuse me for interrupting, Mr. Holmes, but are you aware that expert testimony from independently selected pathologists concurred that the trajectory of the shot which blew off the President's head gave the direction of that shot as coming from the area of the Book Depository?"

"I am indeed aware of that, sir. You refer to the report of the beveling effect observed on fragments of skull brought back from Dallas?"

"I do indeed, sir."

"In my judgment, the beveling is also commensurate with a bullet that exploded the President's head from a position to the right, and slightly forward of the President's car. We would need to look at some detailed drawings I obtained with the assistance of a medical illustrator. We might still disagree, I fear, but then the panel that looked at the portions of skull was not unanimous in its findings."

"There was a minority of one, Mr. Holmes."

"One person can be right, and five wrong, sir, in matters of forensics. But let me repeat: I offer no firm conclusions, only the opinions of an aging sleuth."

"I'm sorry I interrupted. Please continue."

"You will ask me, ma'am, gentlemen, if I can offer a satisfactory hypothesis to link the potential assassin or assassins in the Book Depository to a person or persons behind the wooden fence on the grassy knoll. I can offer several hypotheses but no certain explanations. I must limit myself to two or three of the more prominent ones. We may perhaps begin with Oswald, the person most closely identified with the killing, and held responsible for it. It is said that he acted alone, and it is implied that this was a sudden decision, almost one of impulse, because of his hatred of authority in all its forms, and a frustrated wish to find a place in history. Another hypothesis, linked with this, related the crime to the failure of Oswald's marriage to a Russian citizen who had entered into an affectionate relationship with another married woman, whose marriage was also in difficulties, it would seem. That lady and Mrs. Oswald shared house together in a way that excluded Oswald from his own marriage and family life. There were thus powerful elements present that could impel a man to seek prowess by a reckless, ruthless act which could, perhaps, serve as warning to both those women. If you will, a shot across their bows.

"I have pondered this explanation. It has a seductive appeal, since it provides a sufficient explanation for a terrible deed, and it frees the mind of any need to think further, or to face difficult questions which do not fit with that explanation. I finally rejected it, on a number of grounds. The first one is that to entertain it, we must also entertain the notion that Oswald wished to be a national —indeed an international—martyr. He was sufficiently intelligent, he had shown enough capacity to plan and think ahead, and he had enough experience of such matters as interrogation, in more than one political system, to know that he was bound to be apprehended after murdering the President from an open window at his place of work. He knew with absolute certainty that he was already under suspicion and constant surveillance by the Federal Bureau of Investigation, and thus perhaps by the Secret Service and other intelligence agencies. He had been questioned enough times during the previous two years to be reasonably certain that he would be a prime suspect in Dallas even if the President were murdered some miles from the Texas School Book Depository. That the President should be murdered from that particular building was bound to point immediately and irrevocably to the employee who, above all others, would be under instant suspicion: a Marxist defector to Russia who had since returned to his native land. Oswald also knew, with complete certainty, that his wife and the lady she lodged with had been interviewed at least twice during that same month by agents of the FBI.

"All these factors were surely present in Oswald's mind, so that if we are to regard him as the lone assassin, we must also regard him as a self-appointed martyr, expecting to be arrested almost immediately and accused of the worst crime of the century, with all the forces of law and order and an already elaborate dossier arraigned against him.

"And yet every aspect of Oswald's conduct after the deed, then during and after his arrest, point in the opposite direction to the thesis of the lone martyr. He resolutely and volubly denied all connection with the crime. Why? It is possible, of course, that he had earlier intended to become a martyr, then changed his mind at the last moment, or very soon after committing the crime. In that case, we must ask what was he likely to do? He was hardly likely to stroll through a suburban shopping center. He would surely have hidden himself, laid low or, more likely, fled the city as fast as possible. There is no evidence pointing to any such intention. Instead, he went to his lodgings, changed into casual clothes, and went out for the afternoon, taking no luggage, and with every sign of returning to his lodgings for the night. Despite elaborate arrangements for concealing his weapon, taking it to the Book Depository, and preparing an assassin's lair, it seems he made no preparations whatever for leaving Dallas thereafter.

"I turn from the realm of surmise to the world of fact. Oswald was arrested at 1:50 P.M., in a cinema not far from his lodgings. He had darted in there, according to eyewitnesses, without paying for an entrance ticket, when police car sirens were sounding in the neighborhood soon after the discovery of the killing of Police Officer J. D. Tippit in his patrol car. The scene of that killing is only a few blocks from the Texas theater. Oswald resisted arrest when police entered the cinema, guided there by eyewitnesses who had observed Oswald's suspicious behavior. Oswald was arrested after drawing a pistol on the officers and was taken to police headquarters for interrogation. He was held there from Friday afternoon until Sunday morning, November 24, when he was shot dead by Mr. Jack Ruby in the basement of the police station as police chiefs and detectives were about to transfer their prisoner, using an armored van and a police car to elude reporters and others.

"At no time during several intensive interrogations, identification parades, and an appearance before the press, did Oswald confess to any crime. Rather, he denied all such implications and charges vehemently. We may choose to conclude from this that Oswald was lying, or that he was mentally unbalanced, or a mixture of both. It is possible to sustain that presumption quite far, but not far enough, in my opinion, to establish his guilt in either of the two killings earlier that day. Do we then conclude that he had no part in either killing? I will leave aside the murder of Patrolman Tippit, since that is not my prime concern here, and if Oswald did indeed kill the policeman, that does not establish that he killed the President. It could even indicate that Oswald was innocent of the murder of the President. That is to say, since he had reason to fear the blame might be pinned on him, for reasons that lay with his background, he shot the policeman dead. If he did, that would also explain his behavior in darting into a cinema to escape the attention of passing police cars. These incidents do not confirm that Oswald murdered the President, and I therefore leave them aside, since they point as easily to Oswald's innocence of the major crime as to his guilt.

"We return to the major accusation: the murder of the President. Was Oswald involved, implicated, or connected with it? I believe that he was indeed involved, though not in the exclusive manner asserted by the Warren Commission. Did he fire at the President? I do not know. Then why do I conclude that Oswald was, at the least, implicated in the deed? In part, because the shots from the gun position on the sixth floor window could have been arranged only by one with an intimate knowledge of the book depository, especially the upper floors where cartons were available to form a screen from view elsewhere on that floor, and with a like knowledge, during the previous few days at the very least, of the probable movements of the workforce that day. To digress for a moment, one of the curious facts relating to the assassination is that it occurred at a time when few, if any, of the workforce were present on the upper floors of the depository and none at all on the sixth floor. That is to say, if the President's timetable had been different, part of the workforce then employed in laying flooring on the sixth floor would have been at work, rather than taking their lunch; the assassin would have had no chance of escape, and very little chance of taking up his position undetected."

As Holmes spoke these words, two or three of the company present gasped. A silver-haired gentleman whom I recognized as a senior member of the United States Senate interposed a question.

"You are saying, Mr. Holmes—correct me if I'm wrong—that we ought to be asking just how it was the President came to be passing the book store at a moment when the workforce was at lunch?"

"Senator," replied Holmes, "I must ask that nothing be read into my observations other than that they draw attention to a distressing, but possibly an unavoidable coincidence. The President had a lunch engagement at 12:30. If we encounter a series of coincidences, then we are entitled to further conjectures at the possibility—or otherwise—of such a rash of coincidences. For myself, I confess that I have not proceeded to such conjectures. I would require much more evidence on how and when the President's timetable in Dallas was planned, by whom, who fixed the precise route with its exceedingly difficult bend on Elm Street, at a point where police surveillance appears to have thinned out to a most dangerous degree. And why no surveillance of Oswald's place of work? But others than myself must look into such questions, since I have not had the resources, still less the time, to investigate them."

At this point another member of the assembled company broke in.

"Mr. Holmes, should we now be thinking along the lines of a conspiracy to kill President Kennedy?"

Sherlock Holmes held up a restraining hand.

"Sir, the term 'conspiracy' is somewhat elastic. It may go all the way from two or three men gathered together, almost casually, plotting a possible murder, to a major plot involving scores, even hundreds of individuals, within the country of origin, or abroad, even worldwide. I do not think that we are dealing with anything touching the more extensive levels of such notions, for the simple reason that someone, somewhere would surely have revealed the evil plot before now. The fact that the blanket of silence has continued these many years is best evidence that there was no major conspiracy involving governments. If there was collusion, we must set our sights a good deal below such levels, or perhaps in those regions where secrecy and deniability are a professional calling, a way of life. To continue. Oswald had the required knowledge for arranging an assassin's lair on the sixth floor that morning. It is likely that the final preparations were made some time that same morning. Since the paper bag said to contain the murder weapon was fashioned before the day of the murder, and since it was made of materials identical to those in the shipping room of the book depository, this lends support to the thesis that Oswald was personally involved in the preparations for the assassination. We must also recall the very clear evidence of a fellow employee, cleared of any suspicion, that Oswald brought just such a bag to his workplace on the morning of the assassination.

"But here I must pause, ma'am, and gentlemen. We must note that even if Oswald fashioned the paper bag, and even if he brought a rifle into the depository on the morning of November 22 concealed within that bag, as the Commission concludes, this does not allow us to conclude that Oswald fired at the President with such a weapon, or any other weapon, even though a weapon purchased by Oswald under an alias was found on the sixth floor by the police some time after the assassination.

"The finding and the location of that weapon, bought by Oswald in March 1963 under his alias Hidell, presents some unsatisfactory aspects. It took the police combing the building almost an hour to locate the weapon on the sixth floor of a modest size building, even though the location of the assassin's lair itself was a very prompt and simple matter, given the obvious shield of cartons around an open window giving on to the Plaza. It is difficult to comprehend what the police were doing between 12:35 and 1:22 P.M. on the sixth floor if not searching for a weapon, though it is possible that they assumed the killer had escaped with his weapon, rather than leave the incriminating evidence. But if Oswald did indeed fire the weapon from an open window on that floor in sight of many hundreds of witnesses, it stretches credulity to suppose that he would leave the weapon—his own—on that same floor, barely hidden, rather than attempt to

— 190

hide it, by earlier planning, in some other spot in the building or attempt to escape with it. Unless, that is, we conjure once more the notion of the martyr. But we have already considered the difficulties this thesis presents, and he would surely have left the weapon at the place he used it, not among packing cases at the rear of the sixth floor. A second hypothesis is that he was under the impression his weapon was due to vanish, under some prearranged plan.

"Oswald's palm print was found on the rifle barrel near the forward end, beneath the woodstock, but no identifiable prints were lifted from the trigger, or trigger guard, or the bolt of the rifle. The palm print merely testified to the fact that Oswald had handled the rifle at some time or other—a not surprising surmise. Tufts of fiber were found in a crevice between the butt plate of the rifle and the wooden stock, and these were declared to be identical to those of a shirt worn by Oswald when arrested in the theater on November 22. Yet Oswald changed his clothes when he called at his rooming house at about 1:00 P.M. that day, and we might assume that after a hasty retreat from the Book Depository, covering a walk of several blocks, a bus journey, a taxi journey, and another walk, the first item Oswald would change was likely to be the shirt he wore at work that day. Oswald was meticulous in his laundry.

"These are merely some of the unsatisfactory strands of evidence adduced to condemn Oswald. Other stray pieces of evidence are equally perturbing."

"Could you give us some examples, Mr. Holmes?" It was a ruddy complexioned Senator who spoke.

"I fear I could give a great many, but that would be to detain us for an inordinate length of time, gentlemen.

—191

We may take, however, the evidence of the lady who kept the rooming house where Oswald lodged, Mrs. Earlene Roberts. Even though some four months elapsed between the day of the assassination and Mrs. Roberts's testimony—by which time Dallas had become a city of fear for many witnesses—she nevertheless stated very clearly that at about one o'clock, just thirty minutes after the assassination, when Oswald was in his room changing his clothes, a police car drew up directly outside the rooming house, sounded its horn twice, very lightly, and then moved off immediately. Mrs. Roberts observed the car directly, and though she could not express certainty about the number, there is no doubt of her very clear memory of the police car. A few moments later, she recalled, Oswald left the house in a hurry. Here is one example, gentlemen, of a scrap of evidence that it is difficult to doubt, but which eludes easy explanation. The Dallas police department claimed no knowledge of any such incident from any of their patrol cars that day, though it would have been the simplest of matters to confirm from police records such a significant incident after the shooting in Dealey Plaza. No police officer could possibly forget it, yet no confirmation of the incident came from the police department. It is equally an extraordinary piece of evidence for a rooming housekeeper to invent, thus inviting an undue and unwelcome interest from the police from that date onwards.

"Another example comes from the brief, the very brief moments during that tragic weekend when Oswald was seen by persons other than those interrogating him on the third floor of the Dallas Police Department Headquarters. Deputy Sheriff Roger Craig arrived at the office of Captain Fritz, who was holding Oswald in his office, to report an incident he observed in Dealey Plaza that day, which appeared to link Mrs. Marina Oswald's friend Mrs. Ruth Paine to the scene of the killing. Craig gave a clear description of what occurred in the office at that moment—and you will know, gentlemen, that deputy sheriffs are trained to memorize verbal detail and incidents as a necessary part of their calling. Oswald called out: 'Don't try to tie her [Mrs. Paine] into this. She had nothing to do with it.' Then Oswald half rose from his seat, stared at Captain Fritz, and said, 'Everybody will know who I am now.' A curious remark, which I have pondered a good deal. It may merely mean that Oswald feared his defection to Russia and his subsequent return to the United States would now be known to all and sundry. But if Oswald's intent was indeed to find a niche in history by means of a monumental crime, his alarm is difficult to explain, since notoriety was his chief ambition. On the other hand, Oswald's remark may equally have indicated that some important secret, known only to a few individuals, would be at risk if Mrs. Paine were wrongly identified with any part of what happened in Dealey Plaza that day.

"The explanation of Oswald's remark remains a puzzle, and I place it alongside another curious aspect of Oswald's brief appearances that weekend. In this case, his remarks were witnessed by a large number of journalists, and recorded on television on the spot. When Oswald was brought down at midnight on the Friday for a brief and somewhat chaotic appearance before the press, he stated to the world's press—but also, we should note, before the judge who had arraigned him and the senior police officials who had interrogated him—that he had not been charged with murdering the President, and that nobody had told him anything except that he was accused of murdering a policeman. Oswald then made a plea to the assembled press. He begged, 'I do request someone to come forward to give me legal assistance.'

"Oswald had already made a request for assistance, naming a lawyer at the American Civil Liberties Union in New York City, but he was not able to reach any adviser during the whole of that weekend. Throughout that time, he denied any involvement in the murder of the President, and all who were with him or near him during his interrogations confirmed this. As you know, ma'am, gentlemen, Oswald was subjected to many hours of interrogation. Remarkably, although he was charged with two capital offenses—one involving the President of the United States—the simple device of a recording instrument and the even more familiar and traditional devices of stenography were not available at the central police department. It does not seem to have occurred to any person in responsibility that these were vital necessities, given the supreme gravity of the charges. No record of what occurred during many hours of interrogation has been made available. If any had been available, my efforts on this case could possibly have been more productive and fruitful than I can claim.

"You are, of course, as astonished as I am that some forty-eight hours could pass without the elementary measure of a simple recording device for the crime of the century. And this in the age of advanced technology. What is equally remarkable, however, is that none of the several persons present at the successive interrogations has ever declared in any detail, as a public service, what

Oswald asserted, or admitted, or denied, during that weekend. This blanket of silence during so many years speaks eloquently of some aspect or other of those inter-rogations, but what that aspect is, we have not been told. It is one of many vital gaps in the available evidence, but we may note that studied silence can sometimes speak louder than words. Why did those who interrogated Oswald remain silent thereafter when so many questions came forward in the years that followed? I suggest, ma'am, gentlemen, that this is one of the areas where further investigations are required, if necessary by sub-poena of witnesses.

"But I am not here to discourse on the arrangements within the Dallas Police Department that weekend. You wish me to give my opinion on whether or not Oswald was guilty of murdering the President. Were I to be serving judgment on the case, which thank heavens I am not, I would have to return a verdict of not proven. The most that could be claimed against Oswald would be heavily circumstantial evidence, but not such as to place a verdict of guilty beyond reasonable doubt. Indeed, my further opinion is that the charges lodged against Os-wald as early as Friday, November 22, would not stand up in a court of law operating within the legal system of any free society, on the basis of the evidence adduced and the necessary process of cross-examination of wit-nesses."

At this point a member of the company leaned forward with another question.

"Mr. Holmes, as you know, the very detailed Hearings of the recent Assassination Committee went into a great many of the unresolved problems left by the Warren

Report. Could you say what facts or factors in all these investigations counted most heavily with you in maintaining your doubts?"

Holmes paused. Then he spoke carefully and deliberately.

"If I were asked to select the salient facts that sustained my doubts, I would refer to the shots fired at the President's car, and at least one stray bullet that damaged the paving some distance beyond the limousine. You will recall that only recently, Governor and Mrs. Connally testified before the Congressional Committee to their utter conviction that a shot rang out, which they feel certain hit the President in the neck; then a separate second shot, which hit Governor Connally. It follows that it must have been a third shot, at the earliest, which blew off the top of the President's head, though it could have been a fourth shot if the third shot hit the pavement. Four shots from the sixth floor of the Texas School Book Depository, three of them carefully aimed, strike me as highly improbable, if not impossible, within the given time frames, from Oswald's bolt-operated carbine. Those, sir, are the salient facts that I would select, together with some related imponderables of trajectories, the three spent cartridge cases, their attribution to Oswald's carbine, and the intact bullet found on the stretcher at the Parkland Hospital in Dallas."

15

At mid-morning our hostess rose and invited us to re-fresh ourselves with coffee, which had arrived at a side-table. We stretched our legs, and engaged in conversa-tions of an ephemeral character, then gathered again on the chairs and chaises lounges so that Holmes might continue his disquisition.

"You will wish me to comment further, I think, on the possibility of a conspiracy to murder the President. As I have observed already, the term conspiracy is a very elastic one, stretching from collusion between two or three people, to a grand conspiracy, affecting the secu-rity of the State itself. I do not believe there was any grand conspiracy. But if others were involved, I think that we would do well to turn our attention to the strange and tragic figure of Mr. Jack Ruby. Ruby shot and killed Oswald at 11:21 A.M. on Sunday, November 24, 1963. Of that, there is no shadow of doubt. But noting that fact, a number of doubts and difficulties surround the official explanation of motives, not to mention the singular diffi-culty of explaining how Ruby was able to shoot a heavily guarded prisoner, surrounded by armed officers of the law, and yet not be gunned down by those officers in turn. After all, at such an unexpected turn of events, who could know whether Ruby was, or was not, leading an armed posse, ready to shoot those guarding the prisoner, in some fell design to make off with Oswald, dead or alive? How did Ruby manage to emerge unscathed, apart from swift attempts to disarm him on the spot? Was there foreknowledge of his intention to shoot Oswald in cold blood?

"The motives for Ruby's action are obscure. As advised by his lawyers, he later testified that his chief motives were to avenge the death of the President, and in sympathy for the President's wife and children, so that the widow should at least be spared the appalling necessity of giving evidence at the trial of Lee Harvey Oswald. Killing the President's assassin would obviate that need. But Ruby himself stated later that his attorney suggested this motive to him. Although he was a very impulsive man, Ruby's touching sympathy for the bereaved family did not fit with his behavior, observed by many independent witnesses, at the Dallas police station and elsewhere during that weekend. There, as the world's press and hundreds of strangers jostled for place, Ruby was heavily occupied in handing out invitation cards for his night club, in his familiar, genial fashion. He shared anecdotes with old acquaintances, and though he decided to close his establishments for a brief token period, his feeling for the dead President's family could have been little more than a passing concern that weekend. It was certainly not sufficient to provoke Ruby to risk an attempt on the life of a heavily guarded suspect, arraigned for the crime of the century. But the vital question is this: why was Ruby prepared to risk being shot to death as he advanced with his pistol toward the police officers? Why, unless he was already assured that he would not be gunned down?

"There are other aspects of Ruby's movements that present a mystery. For instance, Ruby's first action on hearing of the President's assassination that Friday was to telephone a near relative to observe, with much consternation, that his, Ruby's, life was in danger. He also promptly remarked to an acquaintance that he would have to leave Dallas. It is difficult to put any explanation to this, other than that some plan had miscarried or got out of hand. Ought we to surmise that Ruby had a part in a plot to wound the President, but not to kill him? Or that Ruby found himself, in American parlance, gentlemen, a 'fall guy' or a 'patsy'—as much a dupe as Oswald, the man he later killed? But if that were so, why did Ruby kill Oswald? Possibly because Ruby was blackmailed into doing so. He may have assisted in the preparations for what turned out to be a crime much more heinous than he had expected; punishable—so far as Ruby in a moment of panic would assume—by death in the electric chair.

"But perhaps Ruby had other reasons for extreme perturbation. Certainly the first news of the shooting brought a very strange reaction from a man habituated to violence of many kinds as he plied his trade in his seedy establishments. Eyewitnesses reported and later testified that he turned very pale, an ashen color, when he first heard of the shootings, and that he sat for a time with a dazed expression in his eyes. Why should Jack Ruby, a product of the Chicago slums, who fought in gangs during his youth, who was on the fringes of that violent underworld—why should he of all people behave thus?

"The answer to this has almost certainly gone with Ruby to his grave. And not only the answer to that vital question. There is very clear evidence that Ruby was at Parkland Hospital soon after the dying President arrived. Two independent witnesses—one an experienced journalist who spoke to Ruby, as an acquaintance—testified that Ruby was there. Yet Ruby denied these encounters. Why should he deny them if his visit was prompted by no more than a citizen's concern for a dying President? Did he have some secret mission or task to perform? Such as placing a bullet on a stretcher inside the hospital, perhaps aware that some time later, the investigating authorities would be baffled by the absence of one of the bullets in the limousine? That they might thus be driven to the hypothesis of a second murder weapon, and a second assassin? Despite elaborate inquiries, many of Ruby's movements during the days prior to the assassination are not accounted for. Equally, some of his movements after the killing are not accounted for. When Ruby was questioned by the FBI three days after the assassination, he refused to give any detailed account of his activities, or the names of all persons he had been in contact with during the previous few days. On Saturday, the day before he shot Oswald, Ruby made several telephone calls. In one of them, which referred to Oswald's transfer, it seems, Ruby observed that he 'would definitely be there': that his interlocutor could 'count on it.' One witness declared that she overheard another telephone conversation that same evening in which Ruby was clearly discussing a weapon of some kind. The witness overheard remarks concerning some plan involving a gun.

"The following morning, Sunday, according to the testimony of a policeman, Ruby entered the Dallas police headquarters at about 9:30 A.M., going up in the elevator to one of the floors where the police officials had their offices. Ruby denied this, but no reliable evidence came forward to locate Ruby at any other place at that time. His movements therafter are not accounted for until he appears at the Western Union telegram office in order to do some routine business. The transactions themselves, date stamped with the time and bearing Ruby's signature, confirm that this was at 11:16 A.M. local time. Ruby then left the building and must have walked the short distance of one block to the Dallas police building, where he gained admittance without being seen, despite a phalanx of policemen guarding all the entrances there. He shot Oswald dead at 11:21 A.M."

At this point one of the company interrupted to put a question to Holmes.

"Do you mind my asking, Mr. Holmes? If Ruby was at Western Union about five minutes before he shot Oswald—and he was in line with other people for business at the counter as I recall—doesn't that point to the Oswald shooting as a sudden, unplanned crime? Ruby couldn't have known they were going to transfer Oswald in the next few minutes."

"Unless, sir, 'they' were waiting for Ruby to be in position before they brought Oswald down to the basement of the police building. That Ruby should be undertaking some casual business on a Sunday morning shortly before the transfer of Oswald was about to take place could equally have another significance. Ruby, and any associates or accomplices he may have had, would recognize that if his assault on Oswald had to appear unpremeditated, Ruby would need a convincing alibi for his movements just before that assault. It would hardly have done for his movements that morning to be traced to the police department itself. That would have pointed the finger in a very compromising manner. What was required was some innocent or trivial errand, preferably nearby, where Ruby would encounter independent witnesses. The Western Union office was only a block away. It was an unusual act of generosity on Ruby's part to have mailed off a money order to one of his dancers on a Sunday morning. Monday would be a more normal day of business for sending, and cashing, a money order. It is possible that Ruby was seeking an alibi to locate himself at a particular place shortly before Oswald's transfer. It is possible that Oswald's transfer was delayed until Ruby was reported to be in a particular position."

Members of the company present again showed consternation on their faces, and once more, Holmes held up a restraining hand. He continued.

"May I repeat, ma'am, gentlemen, that I do not assert that Ruby's movements that Sunday morning are to be explained in this manner. I merely say that they are consistent with a certain interpretation of the evidence. My observations are mere conjecture, within a framework of confirmed facts. I merely suggest that these are as consistent with the known facts as the official explanation of Ruby's movements, and that they help to explain, a little better, how he might have gained, or regained, entry to the police department, where he was a known habitué.

"It is not clear from the official reports precisely when Oswald was brought down from the upper floors of the police building to the basement for his transfer. We do know, from members of the press, that the time for the transfer was changed more than once during that Sunday morning. We also know that the head porter of the police and courts building, Mr. John Servance, was ordered to leave the basement of the police building, along with other employees, on the morning of Sunday, November 24, and to keep the elevator from returning to the basement for a time. It is not clear why this was done. Possibly a safety measure to prevent the gentlemen of the press from gaining access to the upper floors of the police building. Possibly to ensure that the elevator was available promptly at floors other than the basement, as soon as it was required.

"We also know that when the moment came for Oswald's transfer, police officials passed word from the outer ramp in the basement that everything was ready. The precise words used, according to police testimony before the Warren Commission, were: 'Everything is all set.' And again, 'It is all set up.' At the moment Oswald appeared through the basement doors to walk, under heavy guard, the few yards leading to the vehicles, a car in the basement garage let out a loud blast on its horn. It was recorded on television and radio. Perhaps accidentally and unintended. Perhaps a signal. Ruby was standing at the spot where the transfer should have taken place. Ruby acted swiftly. As I have observed earlier, in shooting the prime suspect in the murder of the President, Ruby should have expected to be shot instantly himself by those guarding Oswald, even if he was acting on a sudden impulse. I do not think that Ruby expected to be shot, and I do not think he acted on a sudden impulse."

Several members of the company who sat opposite Holmes looked at each other at this point. There was a pause as Holmes allowed his observations to register. Silence filled the room save for the gentle ticking of an ormolu clock on a satinwood sidetable. At length, a gentleman whom I recognized to be an eminent Justice broke the silence.

"Mr. Holmes, I understand you to say that when Jack Ruby killed Oswald, he was either persuaded to do so, or was acting under orders, or under some threat to his own life, or maybe to his livelihood. Is that what you are saying, sir?"

Holmes looked across, his lips pursed, his long, lean fingers held up before him to form an arch at the tips.

"Sir, I do not know for certain. My trade is to make reasonable deductions from the evidence. In the case of Ruby's attempt on Oswald—and let us recall that no one could be certain that Ruby's attempt would succeed, least of all the assailant himself—Ruby was not the person to act in that manner, at great risk to his own personal safety. Not without some prior agreement or understanding that he would so act, and certainly under severe duress. For Ruby to have planned to murder Oswald when the prisoner was in custody, for Ruby to have acted freely, without duress, meant indubitably that he was also prepared to accept a long jail sentence, closure of his business ventures, and probably financial ruin. In some fashion or other, I believe Ruby acted under duress."

Holmes fell silent once more. The Justice stood up and took one or two paces along the polished floor to the window, where he looked out at the trees stirring close to the window panes. He turned back and addressed Holmes once more.

"What do you think is the balance of probabilities, Mr. Holmes? Just let us have your thoughts. We're not asking for certainties. We know there aren't any. Then we'll take our own decision about where we go from here."

Holmes leaned back in his chair and stared at the ceiling briefly, his chin thrust forward, the aquiline profile etched sharply against the pale lemon walls beyond.

"I can only conjecture. I put it no more strongly than that. But it is possible that Oswald was given a promise of payment or there was some form of undertaking for his willingness to act in some plan or other: perhaps a promise of cash, but the promise may also have extended to freedom from further investigation, or harassment, or both. He might have viewed it as an opportunity to wipe the slate clean if he played a particular role.

"By November 1963 Oswald's political convictions were in considerable confusion. He had tried living in the Soviet Union and came away disgusted with it. His diary and his other writings after his return confirm this. Yet during the summer of 1963 in New Orleans, Oswald was clearly building up his Marxist credentials once more with his 'Hands Off Cuba' campaign on the streets of that city. In his letters to the Communist Party and to radical newssheets in the New York area, Oswald was concerned to draw attention to his arrests and to the resulting publicity, in order, no doubt, to prove his *bona fides* to those who would read his letters.

"To add to this confusion, we may note more recent suggestions that Oswald was trained as an espionage agent by the Russians during his term there and that, later again, he was recruited by the Central Intelligence Agency after his return to the United States. I fancy I hear the question you wish to put. I reply that I do not know, but equally, that the evidence furnished to the Warren Commission by the Central Intelligence Agency —both as to its content and its timing, with a delay of several months in an urgent inquiry—left much to be desired. I do not impute bad motives, nor do I suggest that the Agency lied to the Commission. But I do believe that the Agency was parsimonious with the truth, and neglectful of its duty to furnish all the information that could be deemed helpful to the investigation. *Suppressio veri, suggestio falsi.*

"I think that Oswald may have had some sort of connection with the Central Intelligence Agency, at a very low and occasional level, and I think that the American public should be told the whole truth of the matter. Even if reasons of state prevailed at the time when these questions were first raised, so that any connection was denied in what was held to be the public interest, I think that the public interest now requires that the full truth be known, at whatever cost to the reputation of that Agency—a reputation that it was much too concerned to uphold at the time. The Republic is stronger, not weaker, for knowing precisely what its servants get up to. Agencies should never become a law unto themselves. This applies equally to the Federal Bureau of Investigation.

"But to go on. In late September 1963, Oswald, or someone posing as Oswald, visited the Cuban and Russian embassies in Mexico City to apply for entry visas for those two countries. He sought a transit visa for Cuba, and an entry visa for Russia. Both were denied to him. He had sharp arguments with the embassy officials at those embassies, and returned empty-handed.

"At about this time, a matter of days either way, Oswald appeared at the offices of the Selective Service Headquarters at Austin in Texas, seeking to rectify his dishonorable discharge from the Marine Corps. The employee there was quite certain of the details, and further evidence came from individuals on the spot. The Warren Commission heard, and then dismissed this testimony out of hand, since the witnesses were unsure of the exact date of the visit. Yet the evidence is quite compelling that Oswald did seek to have his dishonorable discharge amended."

At this juncture, one of the guests in the room interrupted Holmes.

"Why is this important, Mr. Holmes?"

Holmes acknowledged the point. "Oswald's earlier dishonorable discharge from the Marines had been signed and approved by Mr. John Connally, when he was Secretary of the Navy. The matter clearly rankled deeply with Oswald. At some time or other he entered in his personal address book the name 'John B. Connally, Fort Worth, Texas. Sec. of Navy.' Mr. Connally was the man Oswald associated with his dishonorable discharge and his inability to gain restitution.

"We should note that Marina Oswald declared in her later testimonies that she was convinced all along that Governor Connally, and not President Kennedy was the target for her husband's gun on November 22. No doubt Oswald spoke of his resentments to his wife before that day and perhaps to others in the Dallas community. Perhaps others worked to persuade Oswald in a plan to fire shots at the Governor when details of the Presidential visit became known and the route of the motorcade was published in the local press in November. If so, that intention could have presented a different opportunity to others."

At this, several of the company stirred visibly, in consternation or confusion. Holmes continued.

"It is my duty to indicate the complexities and intricacies of the case before us; to convey that a number of separate, apparently contradictory hypotheses present themselves. My purpose is to show that of the several plausible hypotheses we might consider, one of the less plausible is that of Oswald the solitary assassin, untouched by the suggestions of others with whom he was in contact, determined to kill the President alone. I have suggested that if Oswald had a personal target for his gun on November 22, 1963, then Governor Connally was the more likely target, and that much of the evidence adduced in the case fits this explanation somewhat better than the present accepted explanation."

"Then why did he fire at President Kennedy?"

"We do not know that he did. If he aimed at Governor Connally, it is possible that the inefficient and badly sighted rifle he used found the wrong target with the first shot. The line of sight from that sixth-floor window made that perfectly possible. He corrected for the second. Equally, someone else may have fired at the President."

"And the third shot?"

"That is the mystery," said Holmes. "I will give you my opinion, based on a detailed survey of the wealth of testimony from eyewitnesses. My opinion is that one shot was fired from the wooden fence on the grassy knoll. It was fired by a marksman with deadly accuracy. The bullet was likely to be one designed to inflict maximum damage on the target, with a shattering effect, rather than a piercing effect. A bullet that would explode on impact, leaving only minute fragments of the bullet. It was not necessary that Oswald should know that a second gun was to be used from a different position that day. It was only necessary that he be instructed in his part of a plan to fire at one or other occupant of the Presidential limousine, not necessarily to kill—since that could not be guaranteed in any case, least of all from a sixth-floor window to the rear. If the object of the attack was to be Governor Connally, Oswald's compliance was reasonably well assured. If he expected to escape detection, he may have fired the shots himself, or he may not. His function may have been no more than to provide the assassin's lair, and to assist his escape. Any carefully laid plan to fire from the sixth floor of a building across a crowded plaza at a closely guarded motorcade would be likely to include such an arrangement, unless the assailant was incredibly foolhardy."

"So where does all this leave us, Mr. Holmes?" It was another elderly Senator who spoke.

"It leaves us with the possibility that the official version of the assassination is at best incomplete, at worst erroneous. There is a need to reconsider the evidence with open minds. In placing my thoughts before you, I felt bound to indicate quite distinctive, even mutually exclusive explanations that fit the evidence."

"You are saying that the case should be reopened, Mr. Holmes?"

"I am only too aware of the vastness of such a task, at this remove. But the American Republic has never been miserly when fundamental matters of justice, of getting to the truth, are concerned."

"What would you recommend, sir?"

"I cannot recommend, sir, since that was not my commission. It is for citizens of the American Republic to recommend."

"But we'd be interested in your views, let's put it that way, Mr. Holmes."

Holmes paused once again.

"There is a case, it seems to me, for a committee of

inquiry that is genuinely independent. I mean by this a body of able men and women who have no formal political allegiances or offices; that is, no special placements in the offices of the state—whether judicial or law enforcing. And such a committee would surely benefit from the expertise of some who have devoted their careers to the complex art and craft of crime detection. It surprises me, if a visitor may be so bold, that several prestigious committees of inquiry have not included in their numbers or membership anyone whose professional training and calling bears directly on the problem to be solved: that is, discovering who committed a murder on November 22, 1963; and discovering how, if not why, a second murder came about two days later in the Dallas police headquarters.

"But there is a further desideratum for any new inquiry, and I fear it is a very weighty one. Such an inquiry needs to be assisted by the prerogatives of the Presidency itself. The agencies we have mentioned in our discussions are the servants of the President, and not of the legislature or the judiciary. Only the President can compel those who serve him to open up their files, and to state the *whole* truth, at whatever cost to the reputation or, to borrow the cant term, the 'image' of the agency. I mean no disrespect to those agencies and institutions that have served the Republic so well for many years now. But it can happen, on rare occasions, that an institution can be overzealous in seeking to preserve its own reputation against accusations of negligence or bad judgment."

"You think we have a case of that here, then?"

"It is possible. Not with malice aforethought. Possibly through inadvertence. It is possible that Oswald was being recruited by one agency for work in countries abroad, yet hounded by another agency, responsible for internal security within the United States—the two institutions unaware of their conflicting designs and purposes in the case of Lee Harvey Oswald. If that unknown conflict of purpose emerged after Oswald was dead, reasons of state might persuade senior officials that the truth had better be buried with Oswald, just as earlier reasons of state required that the nation discover—and discover swiftly—the identity of the President's murderer. There is a line somewhere in Schiller that carries the sentiment, more or less, 'Better a royal lie, than admit confusion in the State.' I believe that members of the Warren Commission eventually took this short cut, with the best of intentions as servants of the Republic. I do not think that they published the truth, the whole truth, and nothing but the truth. Again, I do not think the honorable men who served on the Congressional Committee on Assassinations arrived at the whole truth in this case, despite the expert technical evidence served to that committee by honorable men and women."

At this point an elderly gentleman in the company interposed a question.

"Mr. Holmes, you are aware I'm sure that the Congressional Committee on Assassinations concluded—after sifting a great deal of evidence from the agencies involved—that the CIA, the FBI, and the Secret Service were not involved in the assassination of President Kennedy. What are your conclusions?"

Holmes replied in measured tones.

"Sir, I do not believe that the federal agencies were involved in any way at a formal, or official level. The word *involved* is an elastic term, of course, and I doubt that the appointed heads of those organizations would wish to assert categorically that the vast number of officials in their employ contain no renegade elements. Moreover, those who are professionally trained in the art of what is termed 'disinformation' in the trade, could choose to practice it on their employers by careful planning, especially in organizations where different levels and separate branches are insulated from each other in the interests of security. Moreover, the intelligence community in the United States comprises many elements, as you are aware, sir. The military has its own distinct intelligence networks, and I note that some eight to twelve military intelligence agents were reported to be in place at Dallas on the day of the assassination, though their reports have never been made available. Again, the file kept by the Department of Defense on Lee Harvey Oswald was destroyed some years ago, and the Congressional Committee was unable to ascertain the date of destruction. That seems an unsatisfactory aspect of the Department's affairs, though I do not conclude from this that there is thus evidence of any part in the assassination of President Kennedy."

Our hostess now entered the discussion. Her face registered a mixture of apprehension and some dismay.

"Mr. Holmes, if there were to be a fresh investigation, could you give us your views on possible leads, or directions the investigation might take? Should it start with Lee Oswald, or elsewhere? I do not want to detain you any longer—you have been generous with your time— but I think the question all of us are asking ourselves is: Where does a fresh enquiry start, how does it proceed?"

Holmes now paused for several moments as he gathered his thoughts. The room was completely silent save for the ticking of the clock on a sidetable.

"Ma'am, I will give you what few, tentative conclusions I have formed in a case where the trail has been cold for a good many years now. I believe that Oswald was involved in a conspiracy whose nature and extent he did not fully comprehend. Whether he was merely underinformed or systematically misinformed I cannot say with any certainty. Nor can I say whether Oswald acted under the influence of drugs or other serums administered to him without his knowledge. If that were the case, then I fear that anything could be laid at his door—including an attempt to kill the President.

"As to the other elements present in the killing, I believe that renegade members of the intelligence community in the United States were involved, though at what remove I am not able to say. Why do I assert that they were so involved? Because the case involves some remarkable features—what I might term psychological fingerprints, which are often much more revealing than the more mundane type we associate with investigative work. What are the special features I refer to in this case? The first is the split-second timing, indeed the military precision, of an ambush involving shots from the rear and from the front. The fatal bullet was fired at a moving target, with expert marksmanship, followed by a remarkably efficient getaway, from the grassy knoll to the front, and quite possibly from the Book Depository at the same time, if Oswald played his part in assisting a getaway from that location. Oswald's rifle may or may not have been used to fire shots that morning. Nothing in the evidence of the empty cartridge cases passed to the FBI requires us to believe that Oswald's rifle was used on that occasion for that purpose.

"Another remarkable feature was the speed with which the accusing finger pointed immediately and exclusively to Oswald as a solitary assassin. Not only that, but an ingenious trail of confusion—including the possibility of a second 'Oswald' manufactured during the preceding weeks, or even months—directed the investigators to a number of contradictory directions. The trail of confusion was calculated to lead back to the simple thesis of the one assassin, if only to avoid endless confusion at a time when the American people demanded some sort of answer, if not retribution, for the death of the President. Such a trail had the hallmarks of those who had mastered the techniques, and who possessed the means, as part of their professional calling. Common criminals possess neither the means nor the expertise. The plan was likely to include the provision of false credentials for anyone posing as a Secret Service agent in order to direct people away from areas to the front of the President's car at a crucial time."

"Mr. Holmes," another of the company now put in, "I take it you don't see any connection with the Mafia, then?"

"Of that I cannot be sure, sir. Certainly the underworld had a motive for seeking the death of the President, or at the least his removal. Their prime target was the President's brother, Attorney-General Robert Kennedy, for his determined attacks on organized crime in the United States. Leading figures in the Mafia had vowed revenge, as you know. But if Mr. Robert Kennedy could not be dispatched, why not his brother, whose power of appointment and whose support kept the Attorney-General in his post? When the President's visit to Dallas was announced to the press in mid-September

1963, anyone plotting to kill the President had more than two months to plan and prepare the crime. But how to go about this for the most closely guarded man in the United States? It happened that officers in the CIA were already actively associating with leading figures in the underworld to plot the assassination of foreign leaders, most notably Premier Castro of Cuba. What those irresponsible officers failed to recognize was that their patronage gave respectability to leading figures in the underworld, should they have a separate design of their own, nearer home. And it is possible—tragically so—that the underworld, with its own wide-ranging tentacles, came into contact with extremists in the political arenas of the American South, those who were bitterly opposed to President Kennedy's evolving policy for a rapprochement with Cuba. For its part, the underworld wanted to recover Cuba, where it had enjoyed rich pickings with its gaming tables and bordellos, but much more than that, a safe haven outside the jurisdiction of the United States; a place to store money under corrupt regimes, yet geographically highly convenient for forays to the mainland. Thus, a common cause, and an unholy alliance, between political extremists and their friends in military circles on the one hand, and the world of organized crime on the other."

"And where would Lee Oswald fit into all this, Mr. Holmes?"

"Oswald was known to be in touch with agents seeking to infiltrate pro-Castro movements in New Orleans and elsewhere in the United States, including New York. Oswald's activities were well publicized in the summer of 1963, as they were intended to be. When the President's forthcoming visit to Dallas was announced in September, a unique opportunity presented itself to different elements opposed to the President's policies. Oswald was, in your native parlance, gentlemen, the perfect 'patsy.' He was solitary, easily flattered by attention, he had a degree of cunning, and he was impoverished. He would be told only what he needed to know for his part in any plan. The intelligence community had its files on him. His grudges were known, his background, his thwarted hopes, his political confusion and disillusionments with the two economic systems he had experienced. An ideal candidate for any secret plan."

"But Mr. Holmes, if you'll excuse me"—it was a Senator who spoke—"I can't understand how the top officials in the CIA and the FBI would want to cover up any part their own officers might have played in a conspiracy. Why is there no evidence in the files, why didn't someone, somewhere, come forward in the public interest?"

"That we must leave to further investigation, Senator. I would only say this in conclusion. I think it is very possible that the higher echelons of the federal agencies were also duped. The renegade element may have played them at their own game, with all the professional skills they had learned, and rather more besides. But once Oswald was dead, the agencies had to act to protect their own reputations. Oswald was beyond redemption or redress. Reasons of state demanded that the file be closed, even, perhaps, that portions of the files should be lost, or destroyed, because they might compromise national security and delicate operations elsewhere. The CIA, the FBI, the Secret Service all closed ranks."

The gilt clock on the side table gave out a series of tremulous notes. It was noon. Holmes took out his gold hunter and consulted the timepiece. He rose. The rest of the company stood up. Our hostess raised her hand.

"You will stay to lunch, Mr. Holmes?"

Holmes made a courtly bow.

"If you will pardon me, ma'am, I am certainly overdue in London. I left word with my housekeeper that I planned to return some two days ago. I fear her concern may be mounting."

"Is there some urgent case awaiting your return?"

"None, ma'am. My retirement is much overdue, and I will be moving shortly to a quiet retreat I have purchased in Sussex. I am not the tidiest of men, as Dr. Watson will confirm, and I do not doubt that my good housekeeper has had a difficult passage with my scattered effects this past week."

"Well, Mr. Holmes, I am sure I speak for all of us when I express our thanks to you."

"Not at all, ma'am. I said at the outset that I would not be able to solve this, my last case, and I confess a sense of failure."

Our hostess held up a restraining hand. The elderly Justice with the shock of white hair spoke for the company.

"Mr. Holmes, you have said enough to start some fresh thinking. We're much obliged to you. I think you can leave further developments to us. It's our problem, after all. We ought to handle it."

Holmes shook hands and moved to the door. As we descended the staircase a younger member of the company touched my arm and confided that a special plane would be flying Holmes and myself directly to England, from an Air Force Base in Virginia.

"It will save you going out to Dulles Airport again," he added.

—217

"To whom are we indebted for this favor?" I inquired discreetly.

"I'm not supposed to tell you, Doctor," the man replied. Then he continued, "Let's just say, the plane isn't Air Force One, but it's not much further down the line, same fleet. A friendly gesture. Lunch will be ready as soon as you are aboard."

The limousine awaited us on the road outside. Our farewells were brief, punctilious. We shook hands with the men gathered about the lady whose commission Holmes had accepted. If she experienced any emotion, she concealed it as she offered her hand to Holmes. In a few moments we were in the car and minutes later the Virginia countryside lay about us. Holmes delivered himself of some brief sentiments.

"I feel old, Watson. This is the last time I will see this country. I am ready to go when the old man with the scythe and the hourglass summons me."

I sat in silence. The many years of our association made this a moment of infinite sadness.

We arrived at a United States Air Force Base. The gleaming plane stood on the tarmac at a remote corner of the runway. The blue and white lines of the silver hull, the bold configuration of an emblazoned escutcheon near the nose declared its special associations. Inside, all was comfort: soft pastel colors, deep armchairs, a thick pile carpet. The low hum of the engines moved to a high-pitched whine as we taxied out to the main runway; then, with barely a pause, the vast strength of the engines gathered us up. The plane banked across the white city below us in the sunshine, with its deep brown river, its bridges, the multicolored insects of the traffic moving through the bluff crags of the government buildings. All